Sympathy for the Widow

Jon Athan

For more information on this book or the author, please visit www.jon-athan.com. General inquiries are welcome.

Facebook:
https://www.facebook.com/AuthorJonAthan
Twitter: @Jonny_Athan
Email: info@jon-athan.com

Book cover by Sean Lowery:
http://indieauthordesign.com/

ISBN-13: 978-1985160439
ISBN-10: 1985160439

Thank you for the support!

WARNING

This book contains scenes of intense violence and some disturbing themes. Some parts of this book may be considered violent, cruel, disturbing, or unusual. Certain implications may also trigger strong emotional responses. This book is *not* intended for those easily offended or appalled. Please enjoy at your own discretion.

Table of Contents

Chapter One

October 13, 2002

"Cars are great. They're fantastic. I love 'em, don't get me wrong about that. The *smell* of the hot engine, the *feel* of the steering wheel, the *sound* of the horsepower... I love it! I'm just saying, you can learn a lot by taking the bus, so don't knock it until you try it," Trevor Morrison said, holding one hand up to his chest while grinning like a doofus.

Tall and lanky, Trevor was a twenty-six-year-old car mechanic. He wore grimy blue coveralls and a pair of old steel-toe boots. Soot covered his clean-shaved face and rough hands. His curly black hair was tucked into his navy blue beanie. The glimmer of his baby blue eyes shone through the dirt on his face.

He stood outside of his workplace—a shop called *Alejandro's Auto Repair*. His co-workers, Eddie Martinez and Zach Quinn, stood near the garage. They wore the same uniforms as Trevor. Eddie was short and burly while Zach was tall and skinny.

Eddie said, "Drop the bullshit, man. No one likes taking the bus. You're only saying that 'cause *you* have to take it today."

"I'm not," Trevor said, still grinning.

Eddie huffed and rolled his eyes, then he asked, "What are you going to learn on the bus? Huh? I'll tell you what you're going to learn, man. You're going to learn how many crazies are out there.

You're going to take a–a... What do you call 'em? A...
A census. You're going to take a census of all the
homeless and crazy people out there. That's what
you can do on a bus."

"Maybe I can, maybe I will. I'll start with you two.
How long have you been homeless and crazy?"

"Oh, get the hell out of here."

The men shared a laugh, smiling as they playfully
threw dirty rags at each other. Their laughter
blended with the sound of passing cars on the
neighboring street.

As he recomposed himself, Zach said, "Seriously,
though: isn't it, like, ironic or something? I mean,
Trevor, you work at a body shop, man. Your car
doesn't work, so you're getting it repaired at
another shop *and* you're taking the bus? Really,
man? What's up with that?"

Trevor explained, "Listen, I love you guys, but we
all know you'd just rip me off if I brought my baby
here. Hell, I've ripped off people myself, so I know
you won't do me any favors."

"You have to pay for quality work—and we offer
the highest quality. You know that."

Trevor responded, "Sorry, man, I'm not buying it.
You should try using that line on the next single
mother who shows up here, though. It's a good one."
He waved and walked away from the shop, shaking
his head in amusement. Without glancing back, he
shouted, "I'll see you tomorrow! I have to catch the
bus! I have to dive into the... the *culture* of this
beautiful city!"

"Culture," Eddie repeated mockingly. He shouted,
"Catch the bus, but don't catch anything on it!"

"I won't!"

"You will!"

The men laughed again, tickled by their crass jokes. Eddie and Zach continued bantering as they returned to the garage.

Trevor walked down the sidewalk, smiling and nodding at the other pedestrians. His charisma conjured smiles on all of the other civilians. He approached a bus stop on the next block. He stood at the back of the line, waiting behind seven people—young and old, bored and excited, students and pink-collar workers.

He lit a cigarette and clenched it between his lips, then he pulled his Nokia 6100 candy-bar cell phone out of his pocket. He scrolled down to a name on his contact list: *Naomi Morrison.* He called her.

As he held the phone up to his ear, Trevor took a puff of his cigarette and muttered, "Answer the phone. Come on, answer the phone..."

"Hello?" a feminine voice answered.

"Naomi, it's Trevor. How's it going over there?"

"Hey, babe. We're doing fine. You know, we just *love* being home all day without a car. We *love* it."

"I can sense the sarcasm in your voice, sweetie. I have to tell you: I don't know if I like it."

"Well, I don't know if I like it when you smoke, either. So..."

Trevor lowered the phone to his chest and blew a cloud of smoke over his shoulder. He couldn't help but chuckle.

He held the phone up to his ear and asked, "Who's smoking?"

"Real funny, Trevor. You're not going to be

laughing when you lose your teeth and cough up a lung—*literally.*"

Smirking, Trevor said, "First of all, I don't think you can 'literally' cough up a lung. Secondly, I'm not smoking. I'm just, you know, breathing and stuff. It's smoggy out here, so you're probably hearing me breathe that in." He took another puff of his cigarette while Naomi laughed. He asked, "What did you do today?"

Naomi sighed, then she said, "The same old 'housewife' stuff. I cleaned the house, I did the laundry, I cooked some food, and I took care of our little Riley."

Riley—Trevor grinned from ear-to-ear upon hearing the name. Riley Morrison was their eighteen-month-old daughter. Her sweet image flashed in his mind. She inherited his baby blue eyes and curly brown hair while adopting her mother's freckles and small, soft nose. To him, she was a symbol of innocence and hope. She made life worth living.

He asked, "How's Riley? Is she awake?"

"Of course she is. The girl barely sleeps nowadays. You wanna talk to her?"

"Yeah, put her on."

"Give me a second."

The sound of shuffling emerged on the line. Naomi said something, but her words were distorted. The shuffling sound started again.

In a soft tone, Trevor said, "Riley, it's daddy. Are you there?"

"Dada," Riley said, her voice soft and slurred. She cooed for a bit, babbling and drooling, then she said,

"Cheese!"

Trevor held his hand over his mouth and chuckled. He was overwhelmed with joy. *That's my girl,* he thought.

Naomi returned to the phone. She said, "She thought I was going to take her picture."

Trevor responded, "You should take her picture. Take a lot of pictures. I want one for my wallet."

"Yeah, we can do that. Anyway, um... When will you be home, babe? I miss you."

"You miss me? It's a normal workday. I've been gone for, like, nine hours."

"I know, I know. That doesn't mean I can't miss you, right?"

From the corner of his eye, Trevor spotted a Salvadoran man pacing back and forth near the bus stop. The man was short—five-six on a good day— and bald. He looked young and strong, though. He wore a yellow raincoat over another jacket, black jeans, and matching boots. He muttered to himself in Spanish.

"Trevor?" Naomi said, a pinch of concern in her voice.

Trevor turned away from the man and said, "Sorry, I'm still here. I'll... I'll be there soon. Maybe forty-five minutes, maybe an hour."

"Okay, I'll have a special dinner ready for you."

"I don't think a microwaved meal counts as a 'special' dinner, Naomi."

"Oh, shut up. It's going to be something delicious."

"I'll believe it when I taste it," Trevor responded. Before Naomi could say another word, Trevor said, "Listen, I have to go. The bus will be here soon. I love you."

"Love you, too. Bye."

Trevor disconnected from the call. He looked back at the mysterious man. He couldn't control his curiosity.

As the man approached, Trevor leaned back and asked, "Cómo estás, amigo? Bien?"

The man stopped and glared at Trevor. He breathed sharply through his nose and softly shuddered, clearly flustered. He walked away from Trevor and continued pacing back and forth.

Trevor nodded and whispered, "I was just trying to be nice, bud."

He glanced over at the street and smiled in relief. The bus finally approached. He pulled his wallet out and prepared to board the bus.

***

After paying his fare, Trevor marched to the back of the bus. He sat on the last seat to his left and leaned on the window. He pulled his phone out and sent a few text messages to his friends while occasionally glancing around the bus. He watched as ten people boarded the vehicle. It was emptier than he expected. *At least it won't be cramped in here,* he thought.

He sent a text message to Eddie. The message read: *Hey, man, it's not bad in here. People are people, you should stop being such a judgmental douchebag!!*

As he sent the message, someone sat down directly beside him. There were empty seats all around him, but someone decided to sit on the seat to his left. *Some buffer room would be nice,* Trevor thought.

He smiled and glanced over to his left. He opened his mouth to speak, but he stopped himself before he could say a single word. The smile was wiped from his face.

The Salvadoran man sat beside him. The enigmatic man stared down at his lap and twiddled his thumbs as he breathed deeply through his nose. His mouth moved, as if he were speaking, but he didn't utter a sound. Beads of sweat glistened on his forehead and neck. It was a cool day, but it wasn't exactly cold. Yet, the man wore a raincoat for some reason.

Trevor, surprised and frightened, thought: *stay cool, Trevor, he's just a person like everyone else.* He was an open-minded person, so he never wanted to offend the mysterious man or anyone else.

He coughed to clear his throat, then he said, "I'm sorry if I insulted you with my Spanish earlier. I didn't mean anything by it, really. I just... I know a little bit of Spanish, so I thought it would be useful. Are we good?" The man didn't respond. Trevor said, "My name is Trevor. Okay? What's your name, man? What should I call you?"

The man stuttered, "Ma–Mario Flores."

"Mario Flores. Okay, great. So, Mario, how's it going? What, um... What do you do for a living that you need to wear a raincoat on a day like this?"

Again, Mario didn't respond. His lips flapped, but he didn't say a word. It looked as if he were trying to speak some foreign language. Trevor clenched his jaw and nodded, trying to keep a semblance of control. He figured Mario was ashamed of his work or unemployed. *He's probably at a low point in life,* he thought, *I shouldn't bother him about work.*

As the bus started moving, Trevor said, "It's good to be heading home. I just want to see my family, you know? I want to spend time with my wife, I want to hug my baby girl. Her name is Riley. Not my wife, my baby's name is Riley. I swear, she's the most beautiful girl in the world. She's... She's an angel. Like, a *living* angel."

Trevor was all smiles as he thought about his daughter. His face became neutral as he looked over at Mario. The man remained unresponsive. His blank expression and his quivering lips were difficult to read. He didn't seem angry or sad, though. He didn't glance over at Trevor, either. He just stared down and kept to himself.

Trevor shrugged and shuffled in his seat. He scrolled through the contacts on his phone, planning on calling someone—*anyone*—to get his mind off the situation.

Before he could dial a number, Mario asked, "Do you... know about... the people... in the sky?"

Trevor furrowed his brow and, in an uncertain tone, he responded, "Who? The airplane pilots?"

Mario slowly shook his head and said, "Higher."

"The... The astronauts?"

"*Higher.*"

"I'm sorry, man, um... Are you talking about the moon landing or something?"

"No, no, no. Extraterrestrials. Aliens. Martians. *Gods.* They are the... the people in the sky. They talk to me. They've told me things, *important* things."

Trevor stared at Mario with a deadpan

expression. He didn't know if he should laugh in amusement or cry in fear. He looked over at the other passengers on the bus. Unfortunately, the back of the bus was still empty. He was trapped in the corner seat of the back row, too. *How the hell do I respond to something like that?*–he thought.

Mario said, "The people in the sky... They told me that we have been invited to live with them on a planet called *Juno.* I've seen it in the images that they transmitted into my brain and it's beautiful. It is... *glorious.* You have never seen anything like it before. *Never.* We will be there soon. All of us. There is something I have to finish first, though."

"And, uh... what's that?"

"The people in the sky, they are the good ones. They want to help us because... because this planet has been tainted. You see, there are *bad* ones here. They are the... the subterranean people—the people of the ground. I have to get rid of the subterranean *monsters* before our great voyage can begin."

Simultaneously interested and concerned, Trevor stuttered, "G–Get rid of them? Why?"

"Because they are the *bad* ones. Aren't you listening? The people in the sky can't bring us to Juno if the bad ones are still here. If they do, those subterranean monsters might infiltrate our voyage and invade our paradise. It's like... like... like transporting demons into heaven during the so-called Rapture. I have to stop them. That's my job. They trusted me to do it. They... They told me so."

Trevor loudly swallowed, he licked his lips, and he croaked a few incomprehensible words. He didn't know how to respond to such an absurd story without offending Mario. He certainly didn't want to aggravate him knowing his unstable psyche. So, he smiled and stared down at his lap. *Stay quiet, Trevor,* he thought, *don't get on this guy's bad side.*

Mario leaned closer to Trevor's ear and whispered, "I know you're one of them. I've seen your face before, wicked being. You will *not* invade our paradise. I won't allow it. I am a weapon of the gods. I am the mighty hammer that will strike you down."

Stony-faced, Trevor slowly turned towards the unhinged man. The expression on his face said: *oh, shit.*

***

Mario pulled a pocket knife out of his coat pocket. He unfolded the knife, revealing the three-inch blade. Time slowed to a crawl as Trevor stared at the tip of the blade. The grating noise around him— obnoxious chatter, coughing engines, blaring horns —vanished in an instant. He only thought about his wife and daughter.

Before he could say a word, Mario thrust the blade into Trevor's stomach. The blade easily penetrated his coveralls and punctured his lower abdomen. He pulled the knife out, then he stabbed him again. The second stab cut through his belly button. The third penetrated the area directly under his ribs. Four, five, *six*—he was stabbed six times across his abdomen.

Trevor gasped and writhed in pain with each stab. He felt as if he were being punched by a heavyweight boxer as the blade penetrated his flesh. A stinging pain quickly followed each stab. Geysers of blood gushed out of the wounds, landing on his legs and on the seat in front of him. He instinctively held his hands over the leaking stab wounds on his stomach.

So, Mario stabbed the back of his hands. Trevor's broken bones and torn ligaments could be seen through the gashes on his hands—white in the red. His left pinky was even partially severed, dangling away from his hand. The blood from his mangled hands stained the sleeves of his coveralls and plopped on his legs.

Finally, after the fifteenth stab, the initial shock of the attack subsided and Trevor let out a bloodcurdling shriek. The other passengers glanced back, wide-eyed. They watched in horror as Mario moved up and stabbed Trevor's chest three times. The passengers screamed and ran to the front of the bus.

One elderly woman yelled, "Oh my God! Oh my God!"

The bus driver—a middle-aged man with a frizzy beard—watched the commotion through the rear-view mirror. He was shocked by the attack, but he bolted into action. He honked and tried to pull into the side of the road in a commercial area. The surrounding stores were filled with patrons, though, meaning the parking spaces were already occupied. He called his dispatcher, then he called the police.

As he stabbed Trevor's neck, Mario barked, "You will not infiltrate our group! You will not stain our purity with your wickedness! We will go to paradise! We will visit Juno without *you* or *your* kind!"

As Mario pulled the knife out of his throat, a

stream of blood jetted out of Trevor's neck. The blood splattered on Mario's face and raincoat. His face and clothing were painted red with blood.

As he held his hand over the wound on his neck, Trevor gazed into Mario's eyes and stuttered, "D– Don't... Don't..."

Mario could see the life fading away from Trevor's dull eyes. He heard the other passenger's screaming and sobbing, but that didn't stop him. His mission was his only concern.

He shouted, "I'm saving us! He is one of them, one of the subterraneans!" The passengers still cried and attempted to escape the bus. Mario yelled, "Look! I will unmask him! I will expose the alien infiltrator! I'll do it! Watch me! Watch me, damn it!"

Mario lunged forward and bit into Trevor's nose. With Trevor's nose clenched between his teeth, he growled and shook his head like a dog playing with a chew toy.

Trevor tightly closed his eyes and grimaced in pain, veins bulging from his neck and brow. A wet *crackling* sound emerged as his nose was torn from his face. His nasal passages and part of his septum were severed, leaving his nostrils exposed under a mushy ball of flesh and blood. Blood streamed across his lips and chin, connecting to the blood squirting from his throat.

Trevor hissed in pain and stared at Mario, tears welling in his eyes. He watched as Mario chewed on his nose. Before his very eyes, Mario tossed his head back and actually swallowed his nose. Trevor's mind was flooded with thousands of thoughts, but only one echoed through his mind: *I'm going to die today.*

He was horrified by that fact.

Mario bit into Trevor's face. He gnawed on his left cheek until he tore a chunk of flesh off his face. He sucked on the wound, then he used the blood to help him choke down the flesh. Without any hesitation, he chomped at his face again. He chewed on the ridge above his left eye, then he bit *into* his eye. Blood and a gel-like liquid burst from his ruptured eye—and Mario happily consumed all of it.

While Mario chewed on Trevor's right ear, the bus pulled into the side of the road and the passengers quickly evacuated. Some of the evacuees ran away from the bus, screaming in terror and yelling for help. Others stood on the sidewalk and stared at the back of the bus, falling victim to their morbid curiosity. Pedestrians watched the attack, too.

As Mario severed his ear with his teeth, Trevor attempted to stand from his seat. He was weak due to the pain and his loss of blood, though. He couldn't see from one eye, he couldn't hear from one ear. He felt a warm sensation across his limbs while a cold sweat drenched his body.

He mumbled, "I–I ne–need... to see... Ri–Riley..."

Mario pushed him back down to the seat. He stabbed his thighs. He thought about cutting his ankles in order to stop him from moving, too. His plans were interrupted, though.

The bus driver ran to the back of the bus and yelled, "Get off him! Get the hell–"

He stopped some two meters away from the back row. He was caught off guard by Trevor's condition. In less than seven minutes, he was stabbed and mauled to the point of being unrecognizable. One side of his face was horrendously disfigured. One of his ears was severed. His uniform was soaked in blood. Hot blood blew out of his stab wounds like molten lava from a volcano.

Mario resembled a feral animal. His yellow raincoat was drenched in blood. Blood also covered his mouth, jaw, and neck.

Mario said, "Get back. He's dangerous."

The bus driver lifted one hand up and said, "Put the knife down, sir. Please, don't–"

"Get back, damn it! He's one of the bad ones! He can infect you! Can't you see that?! The gods want *me* to handle this, not you."

"Just put it–"

Mid-sentence, Mario swung the knife at the bus driver. The bus driver staggered back, then he rushed forward. He hit Mario with a few jabs and hooks, but to no avail—his punches were weak.

Mario thrust the knife and stabbed his stomach. He pulled the knife out, then he swung the blade at him, slashing the driver's face. The bus driver lurched away from the back of the bus, horrified. He stopped near the front door and looked back. To his relief, Mario didn't chase after him. To his dismay, he couldn't save Trevor.

The bus driver cried, "I'm sorry..."

He hopped off the bus, holding one hand over his face and one over his stomach. The audience gasped upon spotting his wounds. Some of them rushed to his side and offered some aid.

Mario removed Trevor's beanie, then he bit into his head. Mouth full of hair, he tore a small chunk of his scalp off with his teeth. Trevor finally passed away. The last thing he saw was an image of Naomi and Riley. His lifeless body was slumped against the window.

Mario accomplished his mission, but he couldn't stop himself. He sawed into Trevor's neck and attempted to decapitate him. A three-inch blade could only get him so far, though.

The sound of emergency sirens quickly grew louder as the police approached. The sirens didn't stop him from attempting to decapitate him, though. He gritted his teeth and continued sawing into his neck.

Police officers surrounded the bus with their firearms drawn. The cops took strategic positions, ready to shoot the unhinged man from every angle.

Through the megaphone on a police cruiser, a cop demanded, "Drop the weapon and exit the vehicle with your hands up!" Mario looked out the window and sighed. The cop shouted, "Last warning: get out of the vehicle now!"

Mario released his grip on the knife. The blade remained jammed in Trevor's mutilated neck. The killer casually strolled down the center of the bus with his hands raised above his head.

As he walked down the stairs, Mario shouted, "I've completed my mission! I've... I have *slaughtered* the subterranean being! After I find the others, we will all be taken to Juno! We will finally live in peace!"

"Get on the ground!" a male officer yelled as he tackled Mario.

As he helped his partner, another officer shouted, "Don't resist!"

Other police officers rushed into the bus, hoping to rescue Trevor. There was nothing they could do to resuscitate him, though. He was killed in an apparent act of senseless violence.

Chapter Two

Fifteen Years Later

Mario Flores held a leather tabletop picture frame in his right hand, his eyes glued to the photo it held. The picture depicted himself at a local park with a blonde woman and a blonde girl—his wife and his daughter. His wife was five years younger than him, her blue eyes glowing with youth. His daughter, sweet and innocent, was four years old. She had vibrant hazel eyes.

On the glass of the picture frame, he also saw his own reflection. He was now forty-three years old. He was still short, still strong, and still bald. He worked as a construction manager, earning nearly ninety-thousand dollars a year. Outside of his trailer, he could hear banging, drilling, and whistling sounds along with some shouting.

He shook his head and snapped out of his contemplation. He placed the picture frame on his desk and looked around his small trailer, as if he had just awoken in a different workplace.

Mario muttered, "I have to stop daydreaming..."

He rolled on his leather chair until he reached a file cabinet to his left. He riffled through folders filled with printed emails, budgets, and graphs— *work stuff,* as usual.

The trailer was dimly-lit. Some of the dusk sunshine poured into the trailer through the parallel windows, seeping past the blinds. The trailer had chocolate brown walls and a matching floor. Blueprints clung to the walls like posters of pop stars in a teenager's room. A calendar on the wall behind Mario's desk was open to the month of October.

After two knocks, the trailer door swung open.

George Rivera, a young employee, poked his head into the trailer. He wore a white t-shirt under an orange safety vest and khaki pants. His curly hair was tucked into his hard hat. He had a strong physique, but his face looked soft. He didn't remind Mario of anyone—maybe a former classmate, but no one in particular.

As he looked through the files in a manila folder, Mario said, "Don't tell me there was an accident out there, George. I'm not ready for another one."

"Are you ever ready for one, boss?" George asked, smiling.

"No, I guess not," Mario responded. He closed the folder and looked up at George. He asked, "So, what's up?"

"We were just wondering if you wanted to hit the bars with us after work. We've been doing real good out there, boss. It'd be nice to celebrate, you know? Are you in?"

"Are you inviting me 'cause you want me to cover the tab or 'cause you need me to be the designated driver?"

George chuckled, then he said, "No, no. We're inviting you 'cause we want to get on your good side. And... well, we could use some help covering the tab. These guys, they drink like college kids, but I don't think any of them have ever been on a college campus. Not for class, at least."

The men laughed.

Mario said, "I don't know."

"Come on, boss. You never go out with us. If you want to be a leader, you have to show some leadership. You have to... to create a bond with us, you know? Let's get some drinks."

"I'm not much of a drinker."

"Okay, then you don't have to drink. You might kill our buzz, but... No, sir, you don't have to drink. Hell, like you said, you can just pay the tab and you can be the designated driver if you want."

"So, you want me to be like some confused step-dad on his son's prom night, huh? A provider of free booze and a chaperone?"

"Seriously, Flores, you never drink with us. You come to work every day and you do a great job and all, but you're just... I don't know, man, you're just not with us. Now, I don't like quoting her, but it's like my girlfriend says to me: *'you're distant.'* Don't be like me, boss. Come on. Will you come with us? Just to hang out?"

Mario took a deep breath. He glanced over at the picture frame and thought about the invitation. *No drinking,* he thought, *no matter what, don't drink.*

He said, "Fine. I'm not drinking, though. I've got a busy day tomorrow." He turned his attention to the folder and said, "Finish your shift and be careful out there. I really can't handle another accident. You know I'm squeamish."

"Alright. Thanks, boss."

George closed the door and headed back to work. After a few seconds, an applause erupted outside.

The employees cheered upon hearing the news—
Flores is joining and he's paying.

Mario turned in his seat and shoved the folder into the file cabinet. As he riffled through the other folders, a *buzzing* sound emerged from his desk. He glanced over his shoulder and spotted his touchscreen cell phone vibrating across the tabletop.

The name on the screen read: *Vicky Flores.* And that name always made him smile.

Mario answered, "Hey, sweetheart. How's it going?"

With her soft voice, Vicky responded, "Hey, Mario. I was just wondering what time you're going to be home. I'm making macaroni and cheese for Layla. She wants to wait to eat with you, but I'm telling her you might be busy."

Mario closed his eyes and lowered his head. Layla was his four-year-old daughter—she would be five in three months. He loved her with all of his heart, so he hated disappointing her.

He sighed, then he said, "I'm going to be late tonight."

Vicky joked, "You're not cheating on me, are you?"

"No, no. I just made plans with some of the guys. We're going to a bar."

There was a moment of silence.

Vicky asked, "You're not going to drink, are you? You know it could mess with–"

"I'm not drinking any alcohol," Mario interrupted. "It's just a celebration. I want to make sure these guys know I'm behind them. I want them to know I'm not some... some apathetic psycho boss who will throw them under the bus after the first fuck-up."

"Okay, I get it. I think it'll be good for you anyway. It's good to get out there, isn't it? I have my time with the girls, you should have your time with the boys... Just don't drink, okay?"

"Only water and ice for me, sweetheart. Anyway, how's Layla doing?"

"She's fine. She's finishing that coloring book you got her. You want to talk to her?"

Mario smiled and said, "No, it's okay. Let her draw. I'll be home before nine and I'll tuck her in. I have to go. I love you, hun." Vicky did not respond. With doubt in his voice, Mario asked, "Baby, are you there?"

"Yeah, I'm sorry. I think someone's at the door. I love you, too, hun. Have a good night."

"You too."

Mario disconnected from the call. Still smiling, he placed the phone down on the desk and stared at it. He thought about his family. The thoughts warmed his heart and cleared his mind. Love was the antidote to pessimism and madness, love saved his life and created his future.

He shoved the phone into his pocket. He turned off the lamp, grabbed his coat, then he departed from the trailer and headed to the bar with his employees.

***

The local bar was cold and drab, murky and bleak. The construction workers crowded the bar, drinking and chatting. Some even danced to the smooth rock tunes playing from the jukebox in the corner. Others played pool and threw darts. A few young women—bar-hoppers looking for fun— joined them, too. The mood was cheery, despite the dreary environment.

Mario sat by his lonesome at the end of the bar. He drank water while doodling on a napkin. He drew a sloppy blueprint of a new build. It was the structure of his dreams.

"*Flores!*" George enthusiastically said as he approached the bar. He pushed a stool aside and leaned over the counter. Grinning, he said, "I want you to meet someone, boss. Her name is Denise and she's de-*nice*. She... She really wants to meet you."

Mario smiled and huffed, amused but curious. He knew George was buzzed, but he humored him. George turned and beckoned to a young brunette woman—*Denise.* Denise approached the bar, wearing a tight black dress and matching high heels.

George said, "Denise, this is our boss."

Denise extended her arm forward for a handshake. She said, "It's nice to meet you."

Mario licked his lips and nodded. He was caught off guard by the woman's beauty. Her brown eyes were mesmerizing, her strong, thick legs were attractive.

He shook her hand and said, "Likewise. Um... George said you wanted to meet me?"

Denise shrugged and said, "Yeah. He was talking so much about you. He said you were a great guy, the best boss in town, and he even said you were like a father to him."

"Really?" Mario asked as he glanced over at George.

George said, "*Really.* You've done a lot for me,

'dad.' I figured I could do something for you, too. Why don't you two dance? Huh? It'll be good for you."

"I don't know about that. I'm–"

"Dance! Dance! Dance!" George shouted as he held his mug over his head.

Some of the beer spilled onto his curly hair, but that didn't stop him from shouting. After a few seconds, the entire group started chanting: *dance, dance, dance!*

Mario nervously smiled as he looked around. Judging from George's words—*I figured I could do something for you, too*—Mario started to believe Denise was paid to flirt with him. She didn't seem like an escort, but it was possible.

Denise grabbed Mario's hand and said, "Come on, let's dance."

It's just a little dance, Mario thought, *no big deal, right?* He followed Denise two meters away from the bar. The song on the jukebox changed to a dance track—some pop-rap, made-for-radio song. The couple danced while the construction workers cheered. Some of the construction workers joined the dance, grabbing their partners and filling the floor with their moist bodies.

Mario wasn't much of a dancer. He just swayed left and right while occasionally thrusting his hips forward. He had to stop himself from snapping his fingers. *No one dances like that anymore,* he thought. His eyes widened as Denise rubbed her ass on his crotch. He instinctively grabbed her waist and rubbed his crotch on her ass. He was aroused, he was tempted.

Mario chuckled as he pulled away from Denise. He waved at Denise and returned to the bar, as if to say: *that's enough excitement for one day.*

As he danced with another woman, George shouted, "What happened?! Go dance with her! Loosen up, boss!"

Mario sucked his lips into his mouth and shook his head. He returned to the stool at the end of the bar and continued doodling. He thought: *she's just another woman, it's not worth it.* To his disappointment, Denise joined him at the bar. She leaned over the counter and gently rubbed his hand.

She asked, "Is everything okay?"

Mario said, "I'm fine. I'm not much of a dancer, though. Besides, you'll have more fun with one of these young guys. They've got the stamina that I lost a long time ago."

"We don't have to dance if you don't want to. We can sit and talk and drink."

"I'm sorry, but I don't drink."

"Then... why don't we get out of here and do something else?"

Mario looked up at the woman. He stared at her with a set of inquisitive eyes, as if he were trying to find the sincerity behind her words. He seriously considered her offer, too. *Free, consensual sex with a beautiful woman?*–it was difficult to resist.

Mario said, "I don't... I, um... I'm married, ma'am, and I don't think my wife would appreciate it."

Denise puckered her lips, then she nodded and said, "That's okay. I understand. The offer's still on the table, though. And, if you just feel like talking, let me know. George wasn't wrong about you. You seem like a really nice guy."

"Thank you. Have a great night."

"You too."

Mario was surprised but relieved. He rejected her so he expected a snide response, but she was patient and understanding. *Maybe she wasn't an escort after all,* he thought, *she's just a sweet girl with a thing for older guys.* He snickered at the idea.

He turned in his seat and glanced around the bar. He observed his employees as they mingled with the other patrons and celebrated life. Their joy was beautiful and contagious, causing him to smile from ear-to-ear.

Throughout the night, no one mentioned Mario's violent past. His crime was forgiven and forgotten by society. The memories of the murder never surfaced in his mind, either. He lived the good life.

Chapter Three

A Quiet Night

Mario pulled into the driveway. His black pickup truck rolled to a stop in front of the garage of a white two-story house. His house was located on the hills in a beautiful and wealthy neighborhood. There were at least eighty meters of space between the houses, so there were no neighbors in sight to wave at Mario as he arrived. It wasn't a close-knit community.

Mario climbed out of the car, quietly closing the door behind him. He tiptoed his way to the porch while slowly pulling his keys out of his pocket, then he carefully unlocked the door, so as to not make any noise. He didn't want to disturb his daughter's sleep after all. After successfully entering the house, he closed the door, turned the locks, and sighed in relief.

He took four steps away from the door, then he looked around. The aura of the house felt inexplicably different. For a second, he felt as if he had walked into the wrong house—*a haunted house.*

The first floor of the home was swallowed by a wave of darkness. A door to his left opened up to a storage closet. Next to the door, a staircase led up to the second floor. Farther down that same wall, another door led to a bathroom. An archway to his right led to the kitchen. From over the bar in the kitchen, he could see into the spacious living room and dining area, which were seamlessly connected.

Mario approached the staircase. He stared up at the second floor and loudly whispered, "Vicky, I'm home. *Vicky!*"

There was no response. Mario crossed his arms and rubbed his shoulders. A cold chill cut through him. The silence was deafening and worrisome. *It's nothing,* he thought, *it's nighttime, of course it's going to be quiet around here.* He smiled and nodded, convincing himself that his theory was correct. It seemed like a logical explanation. He walked into the kitchen and turned on the light.

The light poured into the living room from over the bar. The light wasn't strong enough to illuminate the entire living room, though. However, at the other end of the room, a slit of moonlight entered the living room, seeping past the curtains on the patio doors. The moonlight illuminated a sofa and nothing more. The sparkling pool in the backyard could be seen through the slit, too.

Mario grabbed an apple from a bowl of fruit on the kitchen island. As he gnawed on the apple, he checked his cell phone and grimaced. The clock read: *10:42 PM.*

He muttered, "Damn it. Layla's probably knocked out by now and Vicky's giving me the damn silent treatment. She's going to nag at me about this for a week. I should have said ten. Why did I say nine?"

He placed the apple on the counter and stared up at the ceiling. He listened for the usual household noises—creaky floorboards, groaning pipes, rattling windows. He didn't hear anything, though. He didn't even hear his wife's snoring—she purred, actually.

The house was too quiet. He walked back to the stairs.

He said, "Vicky. Vicky, are you home? Layla? Anyone? Anyone at all?" Once again, there was no response. As he walked up the stairs, he whispered a set of excuses to himself: "Sorry, hun, I lost track of time... I ran out of gas in the middle of nowhere... I was taking a dance class."

On the second floor, there was a hallway with seven doors—three on the left, three on the right, one at the end. He peeked into Layla's room, which was the first room to the left.

Layla lay in bed, her back to the door. A head of messy blonde hair protruded from under the blue blanket. The blanket moved up and down as she breathed. It sounded as if she were snoring, too. *Just like her mother,* Mario thought, *sleep tight, angel.* He quietly closed the door and looked over at the last room in the hall—the master bedroom.

Mario muttered, "Damn it, did she just leave her here all alone? What the hell?"

He marched down the hall and entered the master bedroom. To his dismay, the room was empty. The bed was still made up, neat and clean. No one—*no one at all*—had rested on that bed since the morning. As a matter of fact, it looked as if no one had been in the bedroom for hours. The blinds and curtains were still open, the television was off, and the bathroom was empty.

Mario whispered, "What's going on here? Where did you go, Vicky?"

He checked every room on the second floor: the guest rooms, the office, the bathroom and even the storage closet. There was no trace of Vicky's presence, though.

Mario jogged down the stairs, unnerved by the situation. His mind was flooded with dozens of pessimistic thoughts: *is she hurt? Is someone else hurt? Did she leave me?* He stopped before he could reach the front door. A creaky sound, like the sound of an old floorboard, emerged from the living room. *Someone's here,* he thought.

He loudly swallowed the lump in his throat, then he slowly turned around. He gazed into the pitch-black darkness enveloping the living room. He felt a presence in the house, but he couldn't see anyone. He walked into the living room and flicked a switch on the wall. Lights installed on the walls whisked the darkness away while revealing a dark secret.

Vicky Flores sat on a dining chair in the living room. Her arms, legs, and torso were duct taped to the chair. A strip of duct tape also covered her mouth. Blood dripped down the right side of her brow, dribbling across her cheek. A few droplets of blood stained her blue satin nightgown, too. The blood appeared to be leaking from a wound under her blonde hair, which was tied in a bun. She wasn't conscious.

Mario glanced around the living room, eyes wide with fear. He struggled to comprehend the situation. He thought: *a prank? A home invasion? A serial killer?*

As he approached his wife, he stuttered, "Vi– Vicky, wha–what the... What happened, hun? What is... Oh, God, what have they–"

Mario stopped upon hearing a soft creaking

sound behind him. For a second, he froze in fear. He took a deep breath, then he looked over his shoulder.

A woman stood behind him, aiming a stun gun at his torso. She was short, no taller than five-one, but she looked strong—*determined.* She wore a yellow raincoat over a black hooded sweatshirt, black jeans, leather gloves, and matching boots. Her dark auburn hair was tucked into a black beanie, tresses dangling over her brow and ears. She had freckles across her cheeks and nose.

Without saying a word, she squeezed the trigger. The prongs penetrated his chest, sending a jolt of electricity through his body. Stiff like a pole, Mario fell to the floor beside the coffee table. As he shook and snorted, the woman pulled a metal pipe out of her coat. She struck the side of Mario's head with the pipe, instantly knocking him unconscious.

Chapter Four

Introductions

Mario groaned as he awoke, his head slumped down to his chest. His ears rang, his brain throbbed, and his heart pounded. Disoriented and nauseous, he felt as if the room were spinning around him. He felt a warm liquid dripping across the side of his head. *Blood,* he thought, *I must be bleeding.*

He tried to open his mouth to speak, but a strip of duct tape sealed his lips. He tried to stand up, but he was taped and handcuffed to a dining chair. He sat with his back to the kitchen. He thought: *oh, God, what the hell is happening?*

He continued trying to move as he stared down at himself. With each blink, his blurred vision sharpened. He noticed most of his clothing had been removed. He wore a white tank top and striped boxers. His bare feet trembled on the floor, creating a soft, rapid tapping sound. Handcuffs around his ankles also restrained his legs to the chair's front legs.

Mario's muffled cries barely seeped past the duct tape. He lifted his head and stared at the area in front of him. Barely conscious, Vicky sat on the other dining chair directly across from her husband. She faced Mario, her back to the patio doors. A long glass coffee table sat between the couple. There was a sofa to the left and a humongous high-definition television to the right.

Mario called out to Vicky, shouting her name at the top of his lungs, but his voice was muffled by the tape. He even tried to hop forward, dragging the chair an inch with him. Vicky opened her eyes and glanced around. She whimpered as soon as she spotted her husband. The situation was horrifying. Home invasions weren't supposed to happen in her part of town.

"You're awake," a woman said from the kitchen.

Mario stopped crying as soon as he heard her. He didn't recognize her voice, but he knew it didn't belong in his house. He only lived with his wife and daughter.

The auburn-haired woman casually walked into the living room. She wasn't in a hurry, she showed no signs of anxiety or excitement. She sat down on the middle seat of the sofa and stared at Mario.

Mario noticed the sparkle of hatred in her blue eyes. She looked raggedy and disheveled, but she also appeared to be physically healthy. Judging from the fine lines around her eyes, he assumed she was around Vicky's age—late thirties or so. He didn't recognize her face or voice, though. He was looking into the eyes of a complete stranger.

Breaking the silence, the woman said, "You're late. Vicky told me you'd be here at nine. It's..." She shook her arm to move her sleeve, then she checked her wristwatch. She said, "It's past eleven. It's not nice to keep your family waiting. Do you know how *scared* they were? Hmm? I could tell you, but I'd rather let you think about it. The human imagination... It's frightening, isn't it?"

Mario was baffled by the woman's words. He

gazed into her eyes, then he glanced over at his wife, then he stared back at the intruder.

The woman said, "My name is Naomi Morrison. Let me make that clear for you: *Na-o-mi Mor-ri-son.* Do you know me?"

Mario lowered his head, his eyes darting left and right as he thought about the name. *Naomi Morrison,* he thought, *an ex-girlfriend, an old classmate, a former employee?* His eyes widened as the memory dawned on him. He never met Naomi, but he knew about a *Trevor Morrison.* He heard the name hundreds of times in the past, so he connected the pieces. The raincoat finally made sense.

He glanced over at Naomi. He shuddered as she scowled back at him—such a hateful glare. His eyes welled with tears as he nodded.

Naomi said, "That's the response I wanted, but I don't know if I believe you. So, here's what we're going to do: I'm going to remove the tape from your mouth and *you* are going to recount the story of my husband's death. If you lied to me, if you don't remember me and my husband, I will kill your entire family right here and right now. If you scream, I will torture your family, then I'll kill them. Understood?"

Mario breathed rapidly through his nose, overwhelmed by the threat of violence. He thought about Vicky and Layla. *I have to cooperate until I can get my hands on a phone,* he thought, *I can't let her hurt them.* He nodded in agreement.

Naomi said, "Good."

She stood from her seat and approached Mario. She carefully removed the tape from his mouth, folding the strip over on one cheek. Mario gasped for air, then he coughed and groaned. He felt lightheaded due to his injuries. His anxiety didn't help, either.

He stuttered, "Is–Is Lay–Layla okay?"

As she sat down on the sofa, Naomi asked, "Why are you talking about that girl when we had an agreement? Hmm? Do you want me to kill them?"

"No, no, no. Please, no, don't touch them. I–I just wanted to–to know if she's okay. I need to know. Please, ma'am, *please*."

"We'll talk about Layla and Vicky and everyone involved after you tell the story. So, speak."

Mario looked at Vicky and frowned. He didn't enjoy speaking about his past, although Vicky already knew about the crime he committed. He buried the past in the deepest crevice of his brain near the darkest part of his skull. If he wanted to unearth the truth, he would have to enter the darkness—and that frightened him.

Staring down at the coffee table, he said, "Well, a few years ago, I got on a–"

"How many years ago?" Naomi interrupted.

"I–I don't know. I can't, um... I can't remember under pressure. I'm sorry."

"You can't remember under pressure? Well, let me refresh your memory. It was over fifteen years ago. I think it's been around... 5,483 days. Yeah, fifteen years and about a week, give or take a few days. That's how long it's been. So, start over."

Mario grunted to clear his throat, then he said, "Okay, so, around fifteen years ago, I got on a city bus over on... on Fifth Street. I, uh... I sat down next to a young man and I... I..."

"What? What did you do?"

"I killed him."

"*How?*"

Teary-eyed, Mario said, "I stabbed him a few times. I stabbed his stomach, his chest, his hands, his legs, his... I stabbed everything, ma'am. And, I also... Oh, God." He sniffled and shook his head. Tears dripping from his eyes, he said, "I bit his face and his head. I, um... I ate his nose and cheek. I just... I mauled him, ma'am. I acted like a damn animal. I don't know what happened. I just lost control of myself. I'm so sorry. Please forgive me. Please don't hurt my family over this. It was my fault. Okay? I take full responsibility for my actions. I'm... I'm sorry."

Naomi clenched her jaw and fists as she glared at her captive. She wanted to kill him, to pummel his head with the pipe until she could cave his skull in, but she believed that would be too easy.

She said, "I believe you. Your memory is great, Mario. Your storytelling skills could use some work, but you really remembered everything. I thought a 'sick' person like yourself would have had trouble remembering something from fifteen years ago, especially with the drugs and all. It's kinda suspicious, isn't it? We'll get to that later, though."

Mario shook his head and said, "I've been trying to do better. I can remember things, it's just–"

"Be quiet or I'll slit your wife's throat and gut your daughter."

Mario sucked his lips into his mouth and whimpered, horrified by the threat. As Vicky cried on her seat, Naomi grabbed a backpack from behind the sofa. She placed the bag on the cushion beside her. Mario spotted a stun gun, a wrench, and a hammer in the bag. There were more tools in there, too, but he couldn't see all of them.

Naomi pulled a stack of papers out of the bag. She turned her attention to Vicky and said, "I don't know how well you know your husband, but I feel like I should tell you about this—woman-to-woman, wife-to-wife, mother-to-mother. I'm not exactly a wife anymore, but you know what I mean."

Mario said, "She knows everything already, ma'am. Just let her go."

Naomi sighed in frustration. She approached Mario's chair, she muttered something to herself, then she covered Mario's mouth with the duct tape before he could say another word.

She said, "No more interruptions. You'll speak when I let you speak." She returned to her seat, sitting at an angle to face Vicky. She said, "Your husband, Mario, killed my husband, Trevor. Of course, you weren't married to Mario when it happened, but you're married to him now. It's crazy, isn't it? Mario *savagely* killed someone, but, fifteen years later, he's living here in this fancy house with a faithful wife and a beautiful daughter. How did we get here? Huh? Let me tell you."

She lifted the stack of stapled papers and skimmed through the pages. The pages revealed a plethora of information regarding Mario's crime and the subsequent court cases.

As she glided her eyes over the pages, Naomi said, "After the murder, Mario was found to be not criminally responsible for his actions. I remember begging the lawyers and the judge and the jury and anyone who would listen to... to ignore that bullshit, to reconsider that verdict. I threatened them with lawsuits and I begged for justice, but nothing happened. The verdict stayed the same. So, Mario spent eight years in a 'high-security mental health facility.' But, he was still given plenty of privileges during his stay. He could go out for walks, he had supervised visits to the city, then he had *unsupervised* visits, and then he was... he was free. After eight measly years, he was free. No supervisors, no parole, *nothing.* No one is around to make sure he's taking his meds. No one is around to make sure he doesn't eat anyone else!"

She breathed deeply through her nose, struggling to keep her composure. A fire of fury burned in her eyes, hatred pumped out of her heart.

She said, "That's the story. It's absurd, isn't it? This man, *your* husband, killed *my* husband. He destroyed my family and ruined my life... But, he's free to do as he pleases now. For the past seven years, he's been free to live as if nothing ever happened." She tapped her chest with a closed fist three times. She sternly said, "I don't get that privilege."

Vicky felt the pain and anger in Naomi's voice. She couldn't offer her any comfort, though. She couldn't find the words to soothe her pain. She couldn't speak anyway on account of the tape over her mouth. She could only sniffle and tremble.

Naomi stood from her seat. She walked around the living room, examining the picture frames and paintings clinging to the walls.

She said, "Your home is so beautiful. Your family is gorgeous. Your lives are perfect. You're rich, I'm poor. You're carefree, I'm stressed and depressed. You have a career, I have a job. I'm pushing forty and I work at a damn convenience store. I don't have a nice house, I don't have a husband. I don't have any of this!"

She stopped in front of the television. She glanced over at Vicky, then at Mario. She saw the fear in their eyes—and it pleased her.

She said, "I've lived through tragedy-after-tragedy. I've experienced *real* pain, *real* torture. Death haunts me... and I wasn't even on that bus to see it. It's not fair. None of this is fair. You should be... You should–"

She stopped as her voice broke. She choked on her sadness and her sadness opened the door to anger. Tears trickled from her bloodshot eyes with each shake of her head.

She said, "I can't keep going right now. I... I need to relieve some stress before we move on. I need to get this off my chest before I explode and kill one of you..."

Chapter Five

Stress Relief

The sound of creaky chairs and muffled cries meandered through the house. Mario and Vicky hopped in their seats as they sobbed helplessly and mumbled indistinctly. The duct tape muffled their voices, but they still tried to speak. They said something along the lines of: *please don't hurt us, we're begging you.*

Naomi didn't invade their home in order to forgive them, though. She wanted to punish them for their actions. As Mario whimpered on the other side of the coffee table, Naomi approached Vicky, gazing into her eyes. Vicky stared back at her, begging for mercy with her eyes while panting through her nose.

Naomi slapped her with all of her might. Vicky's head flung to the side, causing strands of her hair to dangle over her face.

Naomi said, "You should be ashamed of yourself. You gave this monster a beautiful life, you gave him a reason to live after he took mine!" She slapped her again and, before she could react, she hit her once more. She asked, "Did it feel good knowing you were fucking a killer? *A cannibal?* Did it arouse you, you filthy whore? Did it?!"

Vicky frantically shook her head and cried. Tears streamed down her cheeks, mucus dripped from her nose. The side of her face reddened due to the powerful slaps.

Naomi said, "You're just as bad as him. I have to punish you."

She walked around the chair, then she stopped behind the captive. She glared at Mario with a stern expression that said: *what are you going to do about this?* She grabbed the backrest of the chair, she tilted the chair back on its back legs, then she dragged Vicky towards the patio doors. The floorboards groaned and screeched.

Wide-eyed, Vicky looked every which way. She was amazed by Naomi's strength and shocked by the threat. She looked at Mario, hoping he would save her, but he couldn't do anything about it.

Mario gritted his teeth and screamed at the top of his lungs. He hopped in his seat, dragging the chair a few inches forward. He watched as Naomi dragged Vicky into the backyard.

As she dragged the chair to the edge of the pool, Naomi said, "Look around you, Vicky. Look! Cry! Scream! No one will help you. Your neighbors don't care about you. They never did. They hate you and your husband just as much as I do. Remember that when you're thinking about what you've done."

Naomi turned the chair around so Vicky faced the pool. She grabbed the backrest with both hands, then she crouched and tilted the chair forward. Vicky shook her head and sobbed as her face slowly approached the clean water. She let out a muffled scream, saying something along the lines of: *no, please!*

Naomi dunked Vicky's head into the pool. She watched as Vicky violently shook her head—as her limbs trembled uncontrollably. She counted twenty seconds, then she pulled the chair back.

As Vicky breathed deeply through her nose, struggling to catch her breath, Naomi said, "You've been enabling him. You've been giving him a reason to live. If you never entered his life, he probably would have killed himself already. Instead, you... you tried to 'cure' him with love. You can't 'cure' evil. Now, take a deep breath."

Vicky cried and mumbled incoherently, but to no avail. Naomi tilted the seat forward and dunked Vicky's head into the water again. She counted to thirty.

While Naomi counted, Mario hopped forward in his seat. His knees touched the edge of the glass coffee table. He wouldn't be able to hop through the table, so he tried to jump to the side. *I'll fall over,* he thought, *damn it, I can't get out there.* He could only sit and watch as Naomi tortured his wife with the pool water.

Naomi pulled the chair back, allowing Vicky to breathe. Vicky breathed deeply through her nose as her eyelids flickered. She felt lightheaded, dizzy and confused. The lack of oxygen caused her face to whiten. Each deep breath also caused the chair to groan since her chest pushed up against the tape around her torso. She knew she couldn't free herself, though.

Naomi said, "Let's go for forty this time."

From the living room, Mario sobbed, screamed, and hopped on his chair, acting like a child throwing a tantrum at a toy store. He watched as Naomi dunked Vicky's head into the water. He listened to the *swishing* and *splashing* of the water as his wife panicked. *One, two, three*—each second felt like a minute.

In a smothered voice, Mario cried, "You're... killing... her!"

After forty seconds, Naomi pulled Vicky out of the water. She gently slapped her cheeks, then she patted her chest. Vicky cocked her head back, then she thrust her head forward, as if she were retching. Her nostrils leaked water like open faucets. She lowered her head, barely conscious.

Naomi said, "You're okay. You're fine."

She grabbed the backrest of the chair and dragged her back to the house. She closed the patio doors, secured the locks, and closed the curtains, then she brought Vicky back to her original position.

As she patted Vicky's shoulders, Naomi said, "I had to give you a wake-up call. I needed to let you know that you are *not* innocent in this situation."

She approached Mario's chair, but she ignored his screaming and jerking. She grabbed the backrest of his chair and dragged him back to his original position. Although she struggled a bit due to his weight, she was able to move him.

Mario was also surprised by her strength. *She trained for this,* he thought, *she's been waiting for this for a long time, hasn't she?*

As she sat down on the sofa, Naomi said, "Don't move again, Mario. That will just make me angry. If I get angry, I might do something I'll regret." She pointed at the front door and the patio doors. She said, "I want to make this clear to both of you: no one is going to help you. None of your neighbors will call the police because these rich, pretentious bastards don't give a shit about you. They're knocked out on sleeping pills, painkillers, and other prescription drugs, and they won't wake up. Even if they weren't drugged out, they wouldn't be able to hear anything but gunshots. That's one of the flaws of living in a community like this. It's not really a community at all."

Beads of sweat rolling down his body, glistening in the light, Mario gazed into Naomi's eyes. He tried to analyze her character. He wanted to read her like a book. He already knew she was strong and prepared. Considering she took Vicky outside, he also believed that she was daring. *She has nothing to lose,* he thought. He was horrified by the idea.

People with nothing to lose—nothing to live for—seemed to be the most dangerous.

As she glared back at Mario, Naomi said, "We're going to start slow with you. With what I have planned for tonight, slow is still *very* painful and dangerous."

Mario grimaced and mumbled. The expression on his face read: *oh, shit.*

***

Naomi reached into the backpack. A song of clinking, clanking, and clunking emerged from the bag. Mario could only imagine the types of deadly tools she hid in her backpack. He thought: *she can't fit a chainsaw in there, can she?*

Naomi pulled a steel claw hammer with a rubber grip out of the bag. She stood from her seat and wagged the hammer at Mario.

She said, "I have to take some precautions. This is

going to hurt, but it won't kill you. No, Mario, you can't die so soon. The night's just getting started."

Through the tape, Mario mumbled, "Pl–Please, I– I'm so–"

Mid-sentence, Naomi swung the hammer down at Mario's left hand. Mario tightly closed his eyes and grunted. Naomi lifted the hammer up to her shoulder, then she struck his hand again. She didn't toy with him or even attempt to build the tension in the room. She wanted him to know one thing and one thing only: *this is not a game.*

She repeatedly struck his left hand with the hammer, causing Mario to jerk and convulse on the chair. One, two, three... *fifteen*—she banged the hammer on his hand *fifteen* times, then she stepped back, caught her breath, and examined the damage.

Mario's hand was mangled by the hammer. A wide gash formed across his knuckles, revealing his broken bones and torn ligaments. The skin around the gash was pink and purple. His fingers were broken, twitching involuntarily as blood streamed down to his fingertips. His thumb was spared, though.

A shuddery exhale escaped Mario's flaring nostrils as he stared down at his hand. He was frightened because he couldn't feel his fingers. Pain emanated from his knuckles, reverberating through his entire body, but he could *not* feel his fingers. Numbness was a terrifying sensation.

As she examined the blood on the steel hammerhead, Naomi said, "Stay with us, Mario. If you lose consciousness, your wife and your daughter will take your punishments instead."

Mario glared at Naomi upon hearing the threat. He tried to lunge forward, but the tape restricted his movements and kept him grounded.

Naomi huffed in amusement. She raised the hammer over her shoulder, then she pummeled his right hand. The *thudding* and *crunching* sounds echoed through the room as she hammered him, hitting him another seventeen times. A cut formed across the center of his hand and three of his fingers were broken. His hand turned purple because of the beating.

Veins bulging from his brow, Mario shouted something at Naomi. His voice was muffled, but Naomi recognized the word: *bitch!* It didn't bother her, not at all.

Through her blurred vision, Vicky watched as Naomi knelt down in front of her husband. She watched helplessly as Naomi pounded Mario's feet with the hammer. She even felt the floorboards vibrating under her feet with each blow. Naomi hit him with all of the energy she could muster, releasing all of her anger with the flurry of blows.

Vicky cried and lowered her head. She couldn't stand to hear her husband's bellows of pain. *Why is this happening to us? Why now?*–she thought.

Naomi let out a loud exhale and stood up. She threw the hammer on the sofa and examined Mario's feet.

Mario's feet violently trembled, rapidly tapping the floorboards. Like his hands, his feet turned black, blue, and purple due to the beating. Blood leaked from cuts on his feet, forming small puddles under his soles. His toenails were cracked, too. One of his big toenails had even *snapped* off his foot during the hammering. His feet looked worse than any career ballerina's—bumpy, bruised, *bloody.*

His face as red as a cherry, Mario blinked erratically as he struggled to cope with the pain. He felt as if all of the bones in his hands and feet were broken. It simultaneously amazed and scared him.

Naomi sat down on the sofa and said, "If you somehow break free, rip through the tape and break the handcuffs, you still won't get far with hands and feet like those. You won't be able to walk, you won't be able to fight back. I've pretty much guaranteed that. I hope this stops you from trying anything stupid—for your family's sake."

Mario sneered in disgust as he looked at Naomi. She acted as if she were doing him a favor by breaking his hands and feet.

Naomi continued, "Don't be mad, Mario. You're still alive, aren't you? I can't say that about Trevor, can I? *He* deserves to be angry. *I* deserve to be angry. You? You deserve to be dead. That will have to wait, though. We have a lot to talk about, a lot to do."

Mario sighed and stared down at himself. *We have to overpower her, we have to escape,* he thought, *if she continues to hurt me, I won't be able to do anything.* He cycled through his options, but he didn't have many. He thought about jumping on her with the chair attached to him while his wife hopped out of the house with her chair, but that didn't seem feasible.

He even thought about talking his way out of the situation, but he knew Naomi hated everything about him. He couldn't easily manipulate her. Naomi noticed Mario's silence. She thought he was losing consciousness, though.

She said, "Hey. *Hey.* Remember what I said to you: stay with us or else. If you pass out, your family gets to endure your torture. I don't want to hurt them. Not now, at least. Now, I want to talk about tonight's plan."

Mario glanced over at Naomi. He figured he would buy time by cooperating, so he reluctantly nodded in agreement.

Chapter Six

The Plan

"I'm going to pull the tape off your mouth. The same rules apply: if you scream, I'll torture your family and kill them in front of you. Understood?" Naomi explained, standing in front of Mario.

Mario stared up at Naomi, his body rising with each deep breath. A fire burned in his heart, thoughts of vengeance clouded his mind. *Bite her fingers as soon as she takes the tape off,* he thought, *then tackle her and bite her throat.* He grimaced and whimpered, realizing he would be repeating the past by mauling her. He glanced up at her again and nodded.

Naomi said, "Good."

She pulled the tape off his mouth and folded it over on one cheek. She wasn't bothered by his hoarse grunting and groaning. She walked back to the sofa and took a seat.

Mario wheezed and hissed in pain. He took long, deep breaths, trying his best to compose himself. He looked at his mutilated hands, astonished by the gruesome injuries. He couldn't move his head enough to see his whole feet, but he was able to see his broken toes. He tried to wiggle his toes and fingers, but the effort was fruitless.

"Oh, God, what... What the hell did you do? Why are you–you doing this? Oh, fuck, *why?*" Mario muttered, his voice cracking. He glanced over at

Naomi and cried, "I said I was sorry. I... I apologized. Pl–Please, ma'am, you can't do this. I–I can't feel my–my hands and feet. I need to go to a... a hospital. I need to go now."

Naomi didn't respond. She leaned back in her seat and watched her captive, memorizing the grimace of pain on his face.

Mario glanced over at Vicky and said, "Okay, a–alright. If... If you're going to do this, please leave my–my family out of this." He looked at the stairs and said, "I want to see my... my daughter. I want to say goodbye and... and I want to see her leave this place. She's okay, right? Is Layla fine? Is my baby okay?"

Naomi leaned forward in her seat and said, "She's safe in her bedroom. I restrained her, but I didn't hurt her."

"Will you let her go? Please?"

"No."

Mario sobbed and shook his head, dismayed by the heartless response. His body was drenched in a cold sweat. He felt a strange tingling sensation across his hands and feet as the icy sweat blended with his warm blood.

He asked, "What... What do you want from us?"

Naomi shrugged, then she said, "It's simple, Mario. I want the truth. I want justice. I want vengeance."

"The–The truth? The truth about what? I–I'm not hiding anything from you, ma'am."

"You've been hiding something from everyone, haven't you?"

"No. No, not at all. Wha–What are you talking

about?"

"Are you calling me a liar?"

"No, I'm... Please, just let us go."

He flinched and hissed. A stinging pain emerged from his right hand. His cracked knuckles stung with the slightest movement.

Disregarding his pain, Naomi said, "Here's the plan, Mario. I'm going to torture you until you feel the same pain Trevor felt when you killed him. It's not just going to be for my pleasure, either. No, I'm going to hurt you until I find the *real* reason you killed Trevor because, to be honest with you, I don't believe you're mentally ill. I think you're just a killer who pretended to be crazy in order to kill my husband... and you will likely die for that. Your actions and your honesty will decide if your family dies with you."

Mario gazed into Naomi's eyes. He glanced over at Vicky. The couple shared the same shocked expression. It was an expression that said: *this can't be happening.* They couldn't help but cry as they turned their attention to Naomi. They begged for mercy through their eyes.

Mucus dripping from his nostrils and saliva overflowing in his mouth, Mario cried, "Please don't do this! Please! I'm begging you, ma'am! Let my family go! Let–"

"What did I say about screaming?" Naomi interrupted.

Mario pulled his lips into his mouth, trying to stop himself from crying. Naomi's threats ran through his mind. *She's crazy, she'll actually kill them,* he thought, *I have to protect Vicky and Layla, no matter what.*

He loudly swallowed, then he stuttered, "Pl–Please, le–let my family go. I–I'll do anything. Okay? *Anything.* I am... I am willing to... to repent for my sins."

"Sins?" Naomi repeated in an uncertain tone. She asked, "Have you found God, Mario? Hmm? Has religion saved you?"

Mario responded, "*Yes.* I've been following the word of God for years, ma'am. After that incident, in the hospital, I rediscovered my religion. I live as a God-fearing man."

Naomi narrowed her eyes and examined Mario's demeanor. She analyzed every twitch on his face and every movement of his eyes. Some of the twitches were caused by the pain coming from his extremities, others were due to the anxiety flowing through his body. The man was a nervous wreck. He would say anything to save himself and his family— and Naomi knew that very well.

Naomi stood from her seat. She slowly approached the chair, causing her captor to shudder like a dog after a bath. Before Mario could say a word, she covered his mouth with the tape.

As Mario mumbled indistinctly, Naomi said, "You've lost the privilege to speak... for now." She returned to her seat and said, "I've been watching you and your family for a long time. I think it's been... a year, maybe a year and a half. I missed a few hours during the days when I had to work, but I saw you every weekend. I never saw you go to church. Not once. I've seen you parked outside of bars, fighting the temptation to drink, but I've never seen you at a church. I'll have to hurt you for lying to me, but I have more to say before we get to that."

Mario whimpered and looked down at himself. *I have to get out of here,* he thought, *someone needs to get help.* He bounced up and down on his seat, carrying the chair with him. He didn't get very far, though. As her captive threw a fit, Naomi reached into the backpack. She riffled through the tools for a few seconds, then she pulled a white bottle with a blue and yellow label and a stack of papers out of the bag.

Mario's eyes widened as soon as he spotted the bottle. He glanced over at his wife, seeking a sense of comfort. Vicky sobbed and stared down at the floor, though. She was already mentally and physically defeated.

Naomi shook the bottle and said, "This is Abilify. It's aripiprazole. That's a mouthful, isn't it?" She looked down at the paper and said, "It's used to treat psychotic conditions. It apparently changes the actions of the chemicals in your brain. Have you been taking this drug, Mario?"

Mario nodded and mumbled, unable to say a word.

Naomi said, "Shit. I guess you can't talk with that tape over your mouth, huh? I'll take it off again, but don't forget the rules. I'm really not playing with you."

She stood up and approached the chair. Once again, she removed the tape from his mouth and folded it over on one cheek.

Mario gasped for air, then he said, "Yes. Yes, I've been taking it for years. I won't stop taking it, either.

I promise, okay? You have my word."

"Are you lying to me?"

"No, I swear."

"Are you sure about that? You've lied to me before, Mario."

"I'm *not* lying. I take one tab every night with a cup of water. Every night, okay?"

Naomi glanced over at Vicky and asked, "Is that true?" Vicky nodded rapidly—*yes, yes.* Naomi asked, "And you've personally seen him take this drug every night?"

Vicky stopped nodding. Her eyes drifted towards Mario, then she looked back at Naomi. Truth be told, she didn't see him take the medicine every night. However, she truly believed her husband took the drug without missing a dose. She nodded again.

Naomi smiled and said, "You hesitated. You don't actually watch him take it, do you? He goes into the bathroom with a cup of water or he tells you he already took it, right? Hell, you don't even ask him about it some nights, do you?"

Vicky mumbled something, but, even if she could speak, she wouldn't be able to form a comprehensible sentence. Her mind was addled by the home invasion and the violence. She couldn't rebut Naomi's claim. So, she looked away and sniffled.

Naomi turned her attention to Mario. She said, "Abilify may cause memory loss. Did you know that? It's one of the side effects. I thought about that for a while. You've supposedly been taking this medicine for years. I figured you'd experience some of the side effects and memory loss seemed likely, right?

So, how do you remember the day of Trevor's death so vividly? It doesn't make sense to me."

I haven't experienced memory loss—Mario wanted to explain the situation to Naomi. She was correct: one of the potential side effects of the drug was memory loss. It wasn't a *guaranteed* side effect, though. Regardless, it seemed useless. From the fierce look in her eyes, Mario could see she was stuck in her ways.

Naomi huffed and shook her head, as if she were insulted by something. She walked into the kitchen and dumped the tablets into the sink, then she soaked them with hot water. She crushed them with her fingers, too. The tablets wrinkled and dissolved, then the remaining pieces spun down the drain.

As she dried her gloved hands, she said, "Mario, I think you're willing to take these tablets whenever you think you have to. You'll take them just to prove you're taking them to your wife or doctor, right? You have to keep your act afloat, *right?*" She walked back to the living room and sat down on the sofa. She said, "I can't think of any other reason you'd take that medicine. I'm still not convinced that you were ever mentally ill. You're just another psychopath who wanted to kill."

Mario said, "No, that's not true. I was–"

"Don't interrupt me, you little bastard," Naomi sternly said, scowling at her captive. Mario bit his bottom lip and leaned back in his seat, horrified. Naomi said, "As I was saying, I think you're a psychopathic bastard. You're like those damn idiots who shoot up schools and theaters and then act like their 'sick' after."

Eyes wet with tears, Mario said, "That's not true. I... I don't know what else to say, but it's not true."

"I want you to tell the truth. Admit it: you lied during the court cases, during the psych evaluations, during the treatment. You lied to everyone and used 'mental illness' as a get-out-of-jail-free card. *Admit it.*"

"I was sick back then. I was lost in my own head. The medicine has helped me, though. It really has. I'm a–a better person because of it."

Naomi gritted her teeth and trembled with anger. She wanted to hear *her* version of the truth. She didn't want to hear Mario's tale of self-redemption.

She said, "You're a damn liar. There are millions of people around the world with psychotic disorders, millions more that haven't even been diagnosed, and they don't kill. Mentally ill people aren't violent. No, they... they're not supposed to be violent, goddammit."

Mario furrowed his brow as he watched Naomi. He watched as she covered her face with her trembling hands and muttered indistinctly. She looked as if she were breaking down. *She's not stable,* he thought, *I can break through to her, I can outsmart her.*

In a soft tone, Mario explained, "Please listen to me, ma'am. I'm sorry for my actions. I will regret them for the rest of my life. I *am* sick, though. I lost control of myself that day. And, it's true: most mentally ill people aren't violent. I'm glad you... you understand that. Unfortunately, I was, um... I was part of the small percentage that *was* violent. I'm not like that anymore, though."

Naomi lowered her hands and glared at Mario. She was overwhelmed by her anxiety for a moment, but she wasn't exactly unstable. Mario's speech infuriated her. In her ears, it sounded insincere and condescending.

She responded, "You didn't think it was 'unfortunate' when you ate my husband's face, did you? You didn't think it was 'unfortunate' when you destroyed our family and left us in pieces, did you? Poor you, huh? Poor you... Did you ever think about us? Hmm? Did you?!"

Mario sniffled and said, "I never stopped thinking about that day. I'm sorry. I'm so sorry. Please believe me. Don't do this. You can still leave, we can still get help. It's not too late."

Naomi said, "You're just another psycho killer like all of those other cowards on the news. I will never forgive you for what you did to my family, to Trevor, to our..."

She choked up, croaking and coughing. She covered her mouth and looked away from her captives. Tears streamed down her pink cheeks, but she refused to show weakness around the family.

As she wiped the tears with her sleeve, Naomi said, "It's time to teach you another lesson."

Chapter Seven

An Eye for an Eye

Puffy-eyed, Naomi approached Mario's chair. She covered his mouth with the tape before he could say another word. She returned to her seat and riffled through her supplies. Mario's mind ran wild with the horrifying possibilities. *She'll break all of my bones, she'll cut off my limbs, she'll castrate me,* he thought.

Vicky glanced at Naomi and her husband, cycling between the two. She was still lethargic from the pool torture, but she stayed conscious and attentive.

As she looked through the bag, Naomi said, "You put Trevor through a lot, Mario. You stabbed him over *thirty* times. You ate over *half* of his face. You even ate part of his scalp and one of his ears. I think the one that scared me the most was... was how you ate his left eye while he was still alive. I stayed up for weeks after hearing about that and... and seeing the injury myself. I wondered what Trevor felt and what he saw. It must have been so terrifying for him."

Yet again, Naomi became speechless and stony-faced. A lump formed in her throat—a thick ball that choked her. Mario exhaled loudly through his nose and trembled in his seat. The tragic story of his past made him feel sick. Vicky frowned and cried, saddened by the story. Although she disagreed with her actions, she empathized with Naomi.

Mario tried to say something through the duct

tape. He said something along the lines of: *I'm sorry, please forgive me.*

Naomi wasn't interested in Mario's apologies, though. In fact, she was tired of hearing those damn words—*I'm sorry, I'm sorry, I'm sorry.* That phrase didn't mean anything to her anymore.

Naomi turned her attention to Vicky. Teary-eyed, she asked, "So, can you believe you're married to a cannibal? Can you believe your husband actually consumed human flesh? It wasn't just his eye. He ate his nose... his cheeks... his ear! And he did it while he was still alive!" She stopped and breathed deeply, taking a moment to recompose herself. She said, "He ate him, *he digested him.* And you married him. You gave him the greatest gift in the world: a child. You... You rewarded him."

Vicky wished she could justify her actions to Naomi. She thought: *Mario was sick, but he's better now.* Even if she could speak, however, she knew she couldn't fix their problems. She couldn't repair Naomi's shattered heart, she couldn't change her mindset.

Naomi pulled a tiny white bottle out of the bag. The couple couldn't identify it. The bottle clenched in her hand, she walked across the room, then she stopped behind Mario's chair.

She said, "Mario, if you resist, I'll hurt Layla. Do you understand that?"

Mario gazed into his wife's eyes. He tried to communicate with her. He wondered if she could see Naomi's weapon. To his dismay, Vicky just shook her head and whimpered. As tears flooded his eyes, Mario nodded in agreement—*I understand.* He was willing to endure the worst torture in order to protect his daughter.

Naomi said, "Good. You're a horrible person, but maybe you can be a decent dad."

Naomi grabbed his forehead with her left hand, then she pulled his head back over the chair's backrest. Mario's eyes, wide and alert, darted every which way. He saw the tall, dark ceiling and Naomi towering over him. Naomi held the bottle over Mario's head with the tip aiming down at his face.

Mario still couldn't identify the bottle, but it looked familiar. He heard bits and pieces of his wife's muffled voice. Then, his heart sank as his wife hysterically bawled. He finally recognized the bottle. The thought dawned on him: *it's super-glue.*

Before he could jerk away, Naomi squeezed the bottle. A thick goop of glue fell into his left eye. He instinctively closed his eyes. The super-glue caused his eye to burn, stinging as if lemon were squirted into his eyes. His vision whitened for ten seconds, then it faded to a dark-red color. He screamed as he opened his left eye. He could only open it to a squint and, as he opened it, his eyelashes were plucked. His eye, glazed with glue, became bloodshot.

Naomi squeezed the bottle again, dropping more glue into his left eye. Yet again, Mario instinctively closed his eye. He tried to open it again, but his eyelids were sealed shut.

Naomi walked around the chair until she stopped in front of Mario. She sat on the coffee table and examined his damaged eye.

She asked, "How does it feel to be blind? How did it feel to see it coming?"

Mario said something, but his voice was muffled. Naomi knew it was some sort of insult—'you bitch,' probably.

Mario grunted and groaned as he tried to open his eye again. The effort was fruitless, though. Each attempt to open his eye only amplified the stinging pain. It felt as if someone were holding a flame up to his eye. His eyelids became blood-red, too. As his tears mixed with the quick-drying glue, a white crust formed on his remaining eyelashes.

Naomi said, "It's not over."

A rapid clicking sound emerged in the living room. Mario couldn't hear the sound over his own weeping. Vicky spotted the weapon in Naomi's hand —a retractable utility knife. She screamed at the top of her lungs to warn her husband, but she couldn't break his pain-induced trance.

Naomi said, "You owe me an eye."

She grabbed Mario's chin and stopped his head from shaking, then she thrust the blade downward through the top of his left eye—a clean, horizontal cut. As blood squirted out of the sealed eye, she flicked the handle of the utility knife *up* and nearly cut his eyeball in half through his upper eyelid. The front half of his eyeball, along with his eyelids, popped out of the socket and dangled over his cheek.

Thick strands of dark blood and a clear gel-like substance fell over his cheek and reached his jawline. The gooey strands of blood looked like strings of melted cheese dipped in marinara sauce.

Broken breaths and plenty of mucus escaped Mario's nostrils as he struggled to breathe. He violently convulsed on the seat, causing the chair to groan and wobble. He rapidly blinked his right eye, as if he were in disbelief. He even tried to blink his left eye, but that only caused more gooey blood to drip from the socket. The entire left side of his face tightened and twitched.

Naomi grabbed the front half of the eyeball with her fingertips. She sawed into the eye until it was completely cut in half. She casually tossed the severed half on the ground.

As she examined the damage, Naomi asked, "It hurts, doesn't it?"

Mario stared at her, but he couldn't say a word. He couldn't scream, either. The insufferable pain was shocking. He remained conscious, but he just shut down.

Naomi stepped aside and looked over at Vicky. She asked, "How does he look?"

Vicky immediately sobbed upon spotting her husband's mutilated eye. She retched as she stared into the bloody mush in his eye socket. The strings of gooey blood dangling over his cheek also disgusted her. She felt lightheaded and nauseous.

Naomi said, "Trevor looked worse than this, hun. Imagine if your husband's cheek and his eyebrow were cut off, too. Then, imagine the police telling you that all of those pieces—his eye, his forehead, and his cheek—*were eaten.* Trevor was unrecognizable after Mario was done with him. At least you can still recognize this bastard, right?" She nervously smiled and said, "I can do you a favor, though. Yeah, let me do something for you."

Vicky screamed and leaned back in her seat as

Naomi walked away from Mario's chair. She feared the woman was going to mutilate her eye, too. Instead, Naomi looked through her supplies. After a few seconds, she stopped and grinned.

She pulled a black eyepatch out of the bag and said, "*Ta-da.* This will help us."

She walked back to Mario's chair and put the eyepatch over his left eye, wrapping the elastic band around his head. Streaks of blood still stained his cheeks like bloody tears, but his mutilated eye was finally covered.

Naomi gently slapped Mario's cheek and, in a hoarse tone, she said, "Argh, Mr. Pirate. Don't ye go fallin' asleep on us or yer family will get it. Do ye hear me?"

The pain had sent Mario into a lethargic state. As he listened to Naomi's impersonation of a pirate, he couldn't tell if he was still conscious or if he was dreaming. He couldn't even tell if he was dead or alive. It all seemed so surreal to him.

Naomi giggled, then she said, "I apologize for having so much fun at your expense, but you owed me. Besides, you should be grateful to be alive. I can't say the same about my husband."

Mario breathed shakily as he stared at Naomi. He trembled in pain and gritted his teeth in frustration. He couldn't clench his fists or stomp his feet due to his broken bones, he could only wait and whimper as sweat and blood slowly covered every inch of his body. He thought: *she won't stop after she kills me, I have to save Vicky and Layla.*

Naomi said, "In all seriousness, stay awake, Mario. If you pass out, you'll wake up to a wife without eyes and a kid without a tongue."

Chapter Eight

Our Lives

Naomi walked into the living room, a glass of water in her right hand and a large plastic popcorn bowl in the other. She stopped beside Mario's chair and stared down at him with a set of inquisitive eyes.

She placed the bowl on the table and said, "Same deal: no one dies as long as you don't scream."

Mario looked up at her. He imagined himself smashing the cup on her head, then stabbing her with a shard of glass. The odds were still against him, so he gave her a nod, as if to say: *fine*. Naomi pulled the tape off his mouth. As he gasped for air, she pushed his head back and slowly dumped water into his mouth. Mario happily guzzled the water, relieved and reinvigorated.

As she dumped the water into his mouth, some of it splashing on his nose and chin, Naomi explained, "Don't be confused. I'm not doing this because I've forgiven you. I'm not showing mercy or... or weakness. I just want to keep you awake and strong. My vengeance won't be as satisfying if you're not conscious to experience it. And, if you're not conscious, that will just make me angry."

Mario coughed and spit, unable to swallow the rest of the water. Naomi moved the cup and dumped the water on his face, then she placed the cup next to the bowl. She took a seat on the sofa and waited for her captive to recompose herself. She understood his pain, so she gave him five minutes to cry and revitalize himself.

Mario was finally able to breathe deeply through his mouth. He hissed and he groaned. The water was refreshing, but the pain was never-ending. His feet, his hands, his head—it all hurt.

Out of breath, Mario said, "You... You're crazy."

Naomi chuckled, then she asked, "Is that it? Crazy? I guess you're the expert in that field, right? Come on, Mario, I know you want to call me something worse. What am I to you? A bitch? A whore? A cunt?"

Mario nodded, as if to say: *all of them, you're all of them.* He didn't move his head much, though. He was afraid the rest of his mutilated eye would fall out of his left eye socket, despite the eyepatch. His head hurt because of the torture, too. The mind was a sensitive beast, but it worked miracles to keep him conscious.

Naomi said, "I want to change the subject for now. I loved Trevor with all of my heart, but... it's just too much for my heart to handle right now. I want to talk about you, Mario. What was it like in that mental hospital?"

His voice raspy due to all of the wheezing and coughing, Mario responded, "Are you... Are you seriously asking me that right now?"

"Yes. Answer the question or else."

"O–Okay, um... I... I thought it was hell at first. It was like... like these people, these doctors, they wanted to stop my mission. I was so obsessed with aliens and Juno and... and all of that crap that I actually thought the doctors were the bad guys for a few months. I resisted, but I eventually got better. They helped me. They really did."

"They helped you fake it? They helped you dodge a prison sentence? Is that how they helped you?"

"I didn't... fake it. They helped me understand my illness—*my suffering.* The therapy, the medicine... It all saved my life."

Naomi leaned forward in her seat, her hands on her knees. She stared at Mario with narrowed eyes, as if she were trying to catch him in a lie.

She asked, "Did you have connections in that hospital? Did they help you? Or was it a lawyer or the judge? Who helped you get out of trouble?"

"I didn't fake it!" Mario barked, infuriated.

He grimaced in pain and shook his head as tears dripped from his only functioning eye. He tried to ignore the pain, but it wouldn't go away. Half of his eye was severed after all.

Saliva dripping from his mouth, Mario cried, "Please... Please let me go. I need to go to a hospital. I need to... to see a doctor. I think... Oh, God, I think I'm dying. I don't want to die. Not now, not like this."

Naomi said, "Be quiet."

"I just want to live a–a normal life. I... I want to take care of my wife and my daughter. Oh, my sweet Layla. I want to see my baby."

"I said: *be quiet.*"

Mario continued to mumble about his family while begging for mercy. Vicky joined the orchestra of noise, weeping and stammering.

Naomi shouted, "Be quiet!"

Mario and Vicky stopped. The noise in the room dwindled to some muttering and sniffling.

Naomi said, "I'm not here to play any games. Begging won't save you, so save your energy. Believe me, you're going to need it if you're going to stay awake all night. Now, let's get back to our civilized conversation. Where was I? Where was... Oh!" She turned towards Mario and, as if nothing had happened, she asked, "What was life like *after* you were released?"

Mario glanced around the living room, baffled. He thought: *is this some sort of interview?* He didn't fully understand Naomi's intentions. After so much torture, it was difficult to think straight. He needed a moment to craft the perfect response. He sought to tell her what she wanted to hear in order to gain her sympathy.

His bottom lip quivering, he said, "It was... It was rough. I felt like–like all eyes were on me. I felt... stigmatized, you know?"

"Stigmatized?" Naomi repeated in disbelief. She said, "You can't be stigmatized if you're not actually sick. That's not how it works. Mentally ill people are stigmatized, you... you were just being shunned and punished by society for being a monster."

"I *am* sick, ma'am. I suffer from a psychotic disorder. I, um... I used to hear voices in my head. I saw things that weren't there."

Mario grimaced and groaned as he stared down at himself. The stinging pain from his mutilated eye reverberated across his head and through his entire body. He even felt it in his toes, which he thought he lost during the beating with the hammer.

Still grimacing, he weakly said, "Please call an ambulance. I'll die if you don't. You don't... You don't want to do this. I know what it's like to kill and it's not pretty. It will haunt you for the rest of your life. Please, ma'am, I'm begging you. Call 911."

Naomi stared at Mario with a deadpan expression. She sighed, then she said, "I don't believe you. You're not sick, Mario. Everything you just said, it's just too generic. That's exactly what a phony would say. A pathetic, cowardly phony."

Mario sniffled and muttered, "Why are you ignoring me? I need medical assistance. I need an ambu–"

"Let's talk about work," Naomi interrupted as she shuffled in her seat. She pulled another stack of papers out of her bag, then she said, "You work as a construction site manager, right? You make over ninety-thousand dollars a year and you would have made more next year if it weren't for... well, if it weren't for me."

As she watched her husband and their captor, Vicky thought: *what does she mean by that? Is she actually going to kill him? Is she going to kill all of us?* She tried to speak, she wanted to beg for forgiveness, but she couldn't say a word. Her muffled cries were ignored.

Naomi continued, "Look at this beautiful house, Mario. Look at it. It must have cost you hundreds of thousands of dollars, right? Now, compare this gorgeous house to a studio apartment in Skid Row. Compare it to a homeless shelter in the southside of town. Compare it to those rat-infested, junkie-filled abandoned houses. That's where I've been living. You've been living in heaven while I've been rolling in shit in my own hell!"

Mario flinched as Naomi yelled at him. Her raspy voice drilled into his ears and aggravated his headache. A thought dawned on him as she screamed, though. *It's a grudge,* he thought, *it's not all about vengeance, it's about envy.* He figured Naomi actually hated him because he lived a good life. He believed Naomi wouldn't have pursued her current path if she were dealt a better hand after Trevor's death.

Mario said, "I'm... I'm sorry for my actions. I take full responsibility, despite my... my illness. I am... so sorry to hear about your hardships. I'm responsible for that, too. But, you don't have to live like that. I can make things right. I can give you a... a helping hand. You can live like this, too. Okay?"

Naomi glared at Mario—surprised, angered, insulted. Her eyebrows were pulled close together, her nose wrinkled and her nostrils flared, and her lips trembled with rage. The expression on her face read: *what the hell did you just say to me?* She scooted closer to the edge of the sofa and leaned forward, never taking her eyes off of Mario.

She said, "You act like I think I was dealt a bad hand. You act like this is all just some big misunderstanding. You're basically telling me: *that's life, suck it up.* Then, you slap your money in my face?"

"N–No, it's not like that. I was just saying, we can–"

"Other people may suck it up, they may let the ball roll in any direction, but I've decided to put fate into my own hands. This isn't about an apology, this isn't about money. I want the truth. I want to hear you say this: 'I lied about being sick, I tricked the court, and I'm just a psycho killer.' Say it and make me believe it, bastard."

Mario cried, "I *am* sick. Why won't you believe me? Why won't you just listen to–"

"Break time is over," Naomi interrupted.

As Naomi approached him, Mario yelled, "Help! Somebody help! She's killing me! She's kill–"

Naomi pushed his chin up, forcefully closing his mouth, then she moved the tape over his sealed lips. She gritted her teeth and slapped his cheek five times.

She said, "That was the wrong move, Mario. That was just stupid. I told you: your neighbors can't hear you. Not yet, at least." She glanced over at Vicky and said, "I hope you're enjoying the show, hun. It's going to get a lot bloodier."

As her captives cried, Naomi smashed the glass cup on the table. The cup exploded into a dozen pieces, shattering with a loud *crashing* sound. Mario and Vicky stared at the shards of glass, horrified. They shared the same thought: *what is she going to do with that?*

Chapter Nine

Glass

Naomi held the popcorn bowl up to the edge of the coffee table. She swiped at the shards of glass with her gloved hand, brushing them into the bowl. After she collected all of the pieces in the bowl, she pressed down on the shards with a closed fist and crushed them with her knuckles. She turned the shards into smaller sparkling fragments.

Sweat dripping across his body, Mario stared at the bowl in fear. He looked over at his wife in search of reassurance, but she only cried and mumbled incoherently.

Mario looked back at the bowl and watched as Naomi crushed the shards with her knuckles. He thought about the horrific possibilities. He tried to predict her next move. *She's going to sprinkle the glass into my other eye so she can blind me,* he thought, *or she's going to force me to swallow all of it.* He whimpered and trembled in his seat. He would have hopped, too, but he was out of energy.

Naomi said, "We're going to try something new. It's going to be painful, but it will also be unique. I'll tell you this, Mario: I studied *a lot* of methods of torture to prepare for tonight and I think this one is rare. It's something special."

She giggled as she rubbed her gloved hands on the sofa, trying to get rid of the glass fragments clinging to the leather. She bent over in front of

Mario, pushed his boxers up to his crotch, and then she tapped his bare thighs. His legs were thick and muscular. She thought: *perfect, absolutely perfect.* Her method of torture wouldn't have worked as effectively on thin legs.

As she tapped his thighs, Naomi gazed into Mario's eye and said, "When you attacked Trevor, you stabbed him multiple times in the legs—on his thighs. You didn't want him to get away from you, right? Well, I don't know if they ever told you this, but you actually severed one of his femoral arteries. Even if he somehow survived the mauling and the attempted decapitation, that stab guaranteed his death." She stopped tapping his legs and clenched her jaw. Through her gritted teeth, she said, "So, I won't cut your femoral arteries. I won't let you die, I won't give you the easy way out. You're going to suffer."

Mario sobbed and shook his head. His words were incoherent, slurred and muffled, but he mumbled something along the lines of: *please, don't do this, you'll kill me if you do.* Naomi pulled a sharp chef's knife out of the backpack. She wagged the knife at him—teasing him, mocking him, *tormenting him.*

She knelt down in front of him and said, "Don't move. If I cut that artery, you'll most likely die within a handful of minutes. And, if you die, your family dies with you. Don't move, don't fall asleep."

Mario couldn't help but tremble. He was badly injured and he was terrified. It wasn't an abnormal or unexpected reaction.

Naomi stabbed Mario's right thigh, thrusting the

knife an inch into his leg. She slowly dragged the blade across his thigh while wiggling the handle in order to widen the wound. She stopped before she could sever his femoral artery, though. The horizontal gash was nearly four inches long and two centimeters wide. The cut was wide and deep enough to expose his rugged, ridged muscle.

Blood squirted from the wound and splattered on Naomi's face. Some of the blood even landed in her mouth, but that didn't bother her. She just spat the blood out and moved on to the other thigh.

Mario bellowed in pain as she sliced into his leg. He tried his best to remain steady and composed, but the pain was insufferable. Over the crying in the room, he swore he even heard a *shredding* sound as Naomi widened the cuts—like paper being ripped very slowly. The sight of his wounds caused his stomach to twist and turn, too. He saw every tint of red and even some yellow in the gashes.

Naomi placed the bloody knife on the cushion beside the backpack and examined the cuts. The gashes were nearly identical. They even appeared surgical, clean and precise. She successfully avoided the arteries.

She glanced up at Mario and said, "Now this is going to hurt even more."

She held the popcorn bowl in one hand and then grabbed the puny shards of glass with the other. She held the glittering fragments in her fingertips, and she held her fingertips over the wound on Mario's left leg. She smirked as she stared up at him, as if to say: *do you like what you see? Because I absolutely love it.*

Mario frantically shook his head and stammered incoherently, but to no avail. There was nothing he could do to stop her.

Naomi sprinkled the shards of glass into the wide gash—like sprinkling salt and pepper on a steak. She grabbed more glass fragments in her fingertips, then she sprinkled the shards into the other wound. The glass sank into the gashes and blended with his pulsating flesh. The shards even sparkled in the wounds despite the blood.

Naomi placed the bowl on the table. She gently shoved her fingertips into the gashes and massaged the shards *into* his vulnerable flesh.

Mario violently shook on his chair as he panted through his nose. Pain—raw, unadulterated pain—surged through his body. The shards irritated his wounds and cut into his exposed muscles. The shards stabbed his flesh, creating cuts within cuts. He felt as if he were being stabbed dozens of times with small knives.

As Mario trembled and cried, Naomi smiled and asked, "Do you have any lemon in the house?"

Mario's eye widened upon hearing the question. He had an idea of the next step in her plan. In tears, he shook his head and mumbled.

Naomi sighed, then she said, "You idiot, you fucking idiot... I was testing you, Mario. I've been in your house for hours. I've walked through every room, I've checked every corner. I saw the lemons in the bowl in the kitchen. I'm not blind. Shit, I wasn't going to do this if you told the truth, but I have to do it now. This will teach you a lesson." She glanced back at Vicky and asked, "How can you believe anything your husband says if he's always lying? It's ridiculous, isn't it?"

He's a sweet and honest man—Vicky wished she could utter those words. She could only sob as she watched her husband's torture, though. She felt hopeless and useless.

Naomi entered the kitchen and grabbed a lemon from the bowl on the kitchen island. She threw the lemon in the air and caught it, juggling it like a baseball as she returned to the living room. She cut the lemon in half using the bloody knife.

As she held the halves over his gashes, she said, "Don't lose consciousness."

In a muffled tone, Mario mumbled, "Pl–Please..."

She squeezed the lemon halves, causing the acidic juices to drip into his cuts. Mario tilted his head back and howled in pain, veins bulging from his neck and forehead. Naomi tossed the flattened halves aside, then she rubbed the juice into his exposed muscles with her fingertips. The shards of glass and the lemon juice maximized the pain. He felt as if his legs were on fire.

Mario continued screaming at the top of his lungs. His bellow of pain was loud enough to seep out of the house, but the neighbors couldn't hear it. Vicky closed her eyes and lowered her head. She was emotionally devastated by the brutal torture. Merely thinking about Mario's pain caused her to shudder.

Naomi sat down on the sofa, amused by Mario's screaming. She casually looked through the supplies in her bag, unperturbed by her own vicious actions. She pulled a box of sutures, a needle holder, and a small pair of scissors out of the bag.

Naomi said, "Quiet down, quiet down." Mario continued weeping. Naomi shouted, "Damn it, shut up already! Be quiet! Shit, you act like I ate your face or something. Listen, Mario, do you see this? Huh? Are you listening? Can you see this?"

Mario looked at the small box in her hands. He nodded as he breathed heavily and whimpered, struggling to keep his composure.

Naomi said, "These are sutures. I'm going to stitch you up, but it won't help you very much. The stitches will stop other shit from getting in there tonight, but... Well, who knows how tonight will end? You might end up dead so it might all be for nothing." As she knelt down in front of him, she smirked and said, "For me, these stitches will make sure the pain never ends for you."

Mario furrowed his brow as he stared down at her. He thought: *what does she mean by that?* He watched as she started stitching one of his gashes. At that moment, her plan dawned on him. Naomi stitched the wide cut, pulling together the edges of his flesh, but she didn't remove the glass shards. She left the fragments in the deep cut and ensured the pain would not end until a doctor removed the sutures and the shards during a medical procedure —or until he passed away.

As she stitched his wounds, ignoring the couple's incessant crying, Naomi said, "I'm not a doctor or a nurse, but I read all about stitches online. I watched videos, too. It's amazing what you can learn online, huh? I can learn how to cause the worst pain imaginable, then I can learn how to 'fix' the injuries I create. Anyway, I practiced a bit on chicken breasts, bananas, and plastic, so don't worry too much 'cause that will only increase your blood pressure. You don't want that."

Mario tilted his head back and stared up at the ceiling. He snorted and groaned as he faded in and out of consciousness. He heard his wife's distorted cries—slow and eerie. He couldn't hear Naomi's voice. He didn't know if she was even talking. He still felt the tugging on his skin as she stitched his other wound, though.

Naomi tied the final knot, then she patted Mario's thighs and stood up. She said, "You look tired, Mario. You look... pathetic. I hope you don't fall asleep. If you do, you're going to wake up to a completely different atmosphere in this house. It will smell like death."

Mario, still snorting, lowered his head and glared at Naomi. He only heard bits and pieces of her warning, but he understood the gist of the message. *Stay awake,* he thought, *fight, Mario, fight.*

Chapter Ten

Intermission

Five minutes passed at a snail's pace. Naomi sat on the sofa, her legs and arms crossed. She examined Mario's physical condition, gliding her eyes over his legs and face. Exhales escaped Mario's nostrils in deep, loud snorts. His eyelids were nearly closed, revealing only a slit of his right eye. Vicky remained conscious, but she was still sad and lethargic. She could only cry and mumble as she sat in the living room.

Naomi sighed loudly, then she said, "I think we need a break. More than five minutes, more than ten minutes. I can't keep torturing you like this or you'll die, and it's not your time to die yet. So, here's what I'm going to do. While you rest down here and think about what you've done, I'm going to head upstairs and rest with your daughter, Layla."

Mario, suddenly revitalized, scowled at Naomi. His eye widened, revealing the webs of vibrant red veins across his sclera. He screamed at the top of his lungs and lunged forward, dragging the chair an inch across the floorboards.

His muffled voice seeping past the tape, he shouted, "Don't! Don't hurt her or... or I'll kill you, cunt! I'll kill you!"

Naomi stared at Mario with a deadpan expression, then she burst into a chuckle. She laughed off the threat, tickled by Mario's behavior.

She said, "I'm not going to hurt that little girl, but I will kill Layla if either of you try anything while I'm gone. Just relax and we'll be back to our regularly scheduled program in no time."

As Naomi stood up, Mario screamed and lunged forward again. He dragged the chair another inch forward, but he couldn't reach Naomi. Vicky tried to stand up and lift her arms, trying to rip the duct tape, but she was too weak. Yet again, she found herself only capable of screaming and crying. Horrified, the couple watched as Naomi walked up the stairs.

Naomi stood in the hallway on the second floor. She took a deep breath, mentally preparing herself to meet the child. She opened the first door to the left, then she flicked the switch on the wall to her right. A wave of light illuminated the bedroom, whisking the shadows away. She stood in the doorway and looked around.

The bedroom resembled a typical child's room. Posters of cartoon characters and Disney princesses clung to the baby blue walls. There was a dresser to the left. On the floor beside the dresser, there was a doll house and a toy chest—dolls littered the floor in front of the chest. To the right, there was a short bookcase filled with children's books and coloring books. The room had a peaceful aura.

Layla lay on the bed under the window at the other end of the room. She had twisted her body so that she lay on her back instead of her side. Her eyes were closed. Dried tears stained her pink cheeks. She wore a set of blue pajamas—blue was clearly her favorite color. Her short blonde hair was sprawled across her pillow.

Her wrists were tied together with rope and pulled over her head, then her arms were tied to a bedpost. Her ankles were tied together, too, and her legs were tied to a bedpost at the foot of the bed. A strip of duct tape covered her mouth. She didn't have any visible injuries. She didn't fight Naomi during the initial home invasion.

Naomi's eyes were flooded with tears. She held her hand over her mouth and quietly whimpered. She was overwhelmed by the innocence of it all. That girl, Layla, reminded her of her own daughter, Riley. She took a step forward and staggered as she entered the room. She looked down at her wobbling legs and thought: *what's wrong with me? Why do I feel so dizzy all of a sudden?*

She figured it was the anxiety. She had already seen Layla, she captured and restrained her after all, but the girl still made her feel uneasy and uncertain.

Layla opened her eyes as Naomi sat on the bed beside her. She screamed and shook her head as she squirmed to the other side of the mattress. *Shh*— Naomi shushed her. She caressed Layla's brow, pushing the stray hairs away, then she wiped the crusty tears from her eyes. She lay down on her side next to the young girl.

As Layla whimpered, Naomi softly said, "I'm sorry, hun. I know I told you I'd be back in a few minutes, but... things got out of hand. I lost track of time. You heard screaming downstairs, didn't you?" Layla nodded, tears gushing from her eyes. Naomi frowned and said, "I'm sorry about that, too. I didn't mean to scare you. Can we... Can we talk? Hmm? I mean, if I take the tape off, do you promise not to scream?"

Layla didn't know how to respond. She was taught to scream and run if a stranger bothered her. She couldn't scream with the tape over her mouth and she couldn't run with the rope around her ankles and wrists. She was a young girl, she lacked experience, so she naively trusted Naomi. She nodded in agreement.

Naomi smiled and said, "Good, sweetheart, good."

She carefully removed the tape from over her mouth, folding it over on one cheek. Layla gasped for air and coughed.

The young girl grimaced and said, "My mommy... Where's my mommy? And–And my dad... I want to see my daddy, lady." Naomi reached for her face, hoping to caress her cheek. The girl cocked her head back and cried, "No! Don't hurt me. I didn't do anything wrong, I swear!"

Naomi pulled her hand back and said, "Your parents are downstairs, sweetheart. I'm taking care of them."

"O–Okay. Can I... Can I go? Can I see my mommy? Please?"

"No... No, I can't let you see them. Not now."

"Why?"

A deafening silence befell the room. Naomi thought about her sad life. She thought about her quest for vengeance. She thought about her motives. She believed her actions were justified, but she still felt guilty. Yet, whenever she thought about Trevor and Riley, she felt an irresistible urge to kill—and she couldn't stop thinking about them. She was conflicted.

As tears dripped from her eyes with each blink, Naomi asked, "Do you know what your father did?"

Her voice breaking, Layla responded, "My... daddy?"

"Your daddy. Did he ever tell you what he did when he was younger?"

Layla shook her head. She knew her father's favorite food, favorite color, and even his favorite song. She knew he worked at a construction site— *he built things,* she knew that. She didn't know about his past, though. In fact, prior to Naomi's home invasion, she never thought about it.

Naomi said, "Well, let me tell you the 'short' version—the storytime version. Once upon a time, your father was a monster. He got on a bus, a bus like any other bus, and he sat in the back with *my* husband, a prince named Trevor. Your dad was feeling very, *very* hungry that day. He didn't eat breakfast and he missed lunch, that silly monster. So, he decided to have a snack on the bus. Do you... Do you know what he ate?"

Layla didn't respond. Frightened but curious, she gazed into Naomi's eyes without blinking. The story clearly caught her attention.

Naomi said, "He ate Trevor. Your daddy, that monster, ate Trevor's face. He killed my husband, he killed the father of my daughter. You understand what I'm saying? Trevor is dead because of your daddy. That's the truth."

Layla grimaced and shook her head. She said, "No. You–You're a liar. My daddy didn't do that. He... He's good. He's not a monster."

"It's the truth, Layla. Your dad is a monster in human skin."

"No!"

Layla closed her eyes and whimpered, refusing to believe the horrific story. She thought of her father as a superhero—a knight in shining armor who would protect her from anything.

Naomi pulled a cell phone out of her pocket. She tapped and flicked her finger across the touchscreen, then she showed the screen to Layla. The phone was open to an article on the web browser. The article was titled: *Man pleads not guilty in bus attack.* The picture at the top of the article showed Mario standing in a courtroom, handcuffed and wearing an orange jumpsuit.

Layla couldn't read every word of the article, but she recognized her father in the picture. *Bus attack,* she thought, *just like the big, bad monster in the story.*

Naomi shoved the phone into her pocket and explained, "That's your dad, that's the monster. I saved that article on my phone and I've looked at it every day for years. I tried to find out why your dad killed my beautiful husband. I tried to understand him for so long. How did he stay out of jail? How did he... How did he make a beautiful girl like you? How could something so innocent come from something so evil? I don't know. I just don't know."

Naomi closed her eyes and sniffled. She nuzzled the pillow and sobbed. Her mind was flooded with sad memories—Trevor's death, Mario's punishment, her own torture. She couldn't even think about her daughter without crying. Layla felt her pain. She didn't understand everything, but she felt Naomi's suffering. It frightened her, but she wasn't exactly scared of Naomi.

Naomi gazed into Layla's hazel eyes. She smiled and said, "You remind me of my girl, Riley. I remember when she was your age. Her eye color was different, but... you have that same 'pure' look. Your hair, your eyes, your little faces... It's amazing."

"Where is she?" Layla asked.

As if she were stunned by the question, Naomi repeated, "Where is she?" She loudly swallowed the lump in her throat—*gulp!*—then she said, "She's not like you anymore, Layla. Mario... Your dad changed her."

Layla frowned and cried, "He ate her, too?"

"No, he... he just changed everything."

Tears dripped from Naomi's eyes with each blink. Yet, she couldn't help but smile. Through her blurred vision, it looked as if she were staring at Riley on the bed. For a moment—just a minute—she believed her daughter lay beside her. And, during that short minute, all of her pain was swept away.

She leaned forward and kissed Layla's forehead, then she said, "I'm sorry, Riley. I'm sorry for everything. I should have been there, I should have seen it coming... I love you, baby. I still love you."

Layla was surprised, caught off guard by the emotional gesture, but she didn't fight back. She allowed Naomi to kiss her face and hug her. The pair cried together, releasing their pain through their tears. After a minute, Naomi pulled away from Layla. She wiped the tears from her cheeks, then she cleaned the girl's face.

She said, "I'm sorry for everything I've put you through. I'm just trying to make everything right. I'm... I'm trying to 'fix' your dad. I'm trying to, um... to make a statement. Don't be scared, baby. Just close your eyes and tell yourself: 'it will all be over soon.' I promise, I'll try to make it easy for everyone."

Her lips trembling, Layla asked, "Can I go now? Please? I want my mommy, I want–"

Mid-sentence, Naomi covered her mouth with the tape. Layla tried to speak, but her effort was fruitless. Naomi stared at her with a set of despondent eyes, as if it were the last time she would ever see her. She kissed Layla's forehead once more—a long, affectionate kiss.

She said, "Goodbye, baby. Stay strong."

As Layla squirmed on the bed, Naomi walked to the door. She had to fight the urge to release her. *She's not Riley, don't let her go,* she thought, *you need her, he needs her.* Without looking back at the child, she turned off the light and exited the room, quietly closing the door behind her.

Chapter Eleven

Without Trust

Naomi stood at the top of the stairs. She rubbed her eyes and drew long, deep breaths, trying her best to recompose herself in order to keep a semblance of power and control. She didn't want to appear weak or vulnerable around Mario. *He's smart, he's evil, he's dangerous,* she thought, *I can't let him overpower me, physically or mentally.*

From the top of the stairs, she could hear the sound of furniture screeching on the floorboards. She forced a smile and headed down.

"Oh, you idiots. You fucking idiots," she said as she reached the bottom of the stairs.

Naomi placed her hands on her hips and tapped her foot, like a disappointed mother. Mario had moved across the living room with the chair attached to him. He moved past the sofa and almost reached the console table next to the staircase. Vicky, on the other hand, hopped across the room with her chair in an attempt to reach the patio doors.

His sweat-soaked tank top clinging to his body, Mario frantically shook his head and shouted. His shout was muffled by the wrinkled tape over his mouth, though. He said something along the lines of: *if you touched her, I'm going to kill you!*

Naomi wasn't bothered by the threat. She expected it after all. She walked in front of Mario and examined the console table. Picture frames, flower vases, envelopes, a lamp, *a telephone*—her eyes stopped on the cordless landline phone.

Clearly, Mario tried to reach the phone to call for help despite the tape over his mouth. Naomi grabbed the phone and shoved it into her pocket. As Mario screamed and squirmed, she grabbed the back of his chair, then she spun him around so that he faced the living room again.

She said, "You shouldn't bounce around like that Mario. You'll end up ruining those stitches and you know I worked hard on that." She nodded at Vicky and said, "You touch that door and I cut your daughter's head off. You hear me?"

Vicky lowered her head and sobbed. She was a meter away from the patio door—*a mere meter.* She could have leaned forward and hurled herself through the glass door, causing a loud *crashing* sound that could have awakened her neighbors. She could have ended the nightmare. She couldn't jeopardize her daughter's safety, though.

Naomi walked across the spacious living room, the landline phone in her right hand. She stopped at the other end of the room, between the television and the kitchen archway. She stood at least ten meters away from Mario and Vicky. She sneered in disgust as she examined the couple. She thought: *untrustworthy, selfish, despicable, disgusting.*

She wagged the phone at Mario and said, "I didn't hurt, Layla. No, I didn't harm a hair on her pretty little head. I kept my end of the deal, but you didn't. I asked you to wait down here and rest. That's all, that's it. Instead, you tried to call for help while your wife tried to break out. How could I ever trust you again?"

Mario tried to speak, but his words were muffled. He couldn't think of a decent excuse anyway. He was caught red-handed.

Naomi said, "If I can't trust you to relax, then I can't trust you to *honestly* answer tonight's big question: are you really sick or are you just a crazy killer?"

Naomi clicked her tongue, then she sighed in disappointment. A smile stretched across her face as she examined Mario's injuries. The duct tape stopped him from speaking while also restricting his movement. Most of his fingers were broken, too, protruding every which way. Some blood gushed out of the gashes on his thighs, oozing past the sutures.

She said, "You weren't going to be able to call anyone with those hands anyway. What a stupid way to break our trust... It was all for nothing, Mario. Let me prove it to you."

Mario watched as Naomi dialed a number on the phone. He listened to every tone from the keypad, counting each number—one, two, *three.* Only one three-digit phone number echoed through his head: *911.* A bloody tear rolled down his left cheek as he narrowed his right eye and tilted his head to the side. *Is she actually doing this? Is she crazy?*–he thought.

Naomi put the phone on speaker, then she held it out so it faced Mario. She mouthed: *now's your chance.*

Through the speaker, a female operator asked, "911, what is the location of your emergency?"

In disbelief, Mario and Vicky looked at each other as they listened to the voice. They were shocked by their captor's ballsy move. It was as if Naomi wanted to get caught—as if she wanted to be stopped.

The operator asked, "Hello? Can you hear me?"

Mario and Vicky simultaneously turned towards Naomi. They screamed at the top of their lungs, trying their best to call for help. Veins bulged from their red necks. They felt tingly sensations in their throats, as if ants were scurrying down to their stomachs. They feared their vocal cords would rupture, but they couldn't stop themselves. The shouting and crying was loud, but their muffled voices sounded faint over the phone.

Mario tried to hop forward with his chair, but he was weak and exhausted. He exerted all of his energy while trying to reach the console table earlier. Vicky scooted a few inches forward, but she was still farther away from the phone than her husband. From her warped, hopeless perspective, she felt like Naomi was a mile away from her.

"What is the nature of your emergency?" the operator asked.

Naomi held her other hand over her mouth and snickered. She stepped in reverse until her back hit the wall, moving farther away from the desperate couple.

As if she were speaking to someone else—a co-worker or a supervisor, maybe—the operator said, "I can't hear a thing. It sounds like a pocket dial, but it's a landline. Probably a kid."

In a muffled tone, Mario shouted, "No! Damn it, no!"

The call disconnected.

Naomi said, "I told you: it was all for nothing."

She removed the rechargeable battery, then she placed the phone on the kitchen bar. She threw the battery at the patio doors.

"They probably have your address now since it's a landline phone, but they're not coming here," she said. "No, no, no. They'll try to call again, but only the phone in your bedroom will ring. When you don't answer, they'll leave a voicemail and move on. In the morning, after your neighbors wake up and start hearing all of the noise, that's when the police will show up. We have plenty of time until then."

Mario sighed in disappointment. He glanced over his shoulder and stared at the staircase. He thought about Layla. He regretted his attempt to call for help. He wondered if he killed his daughter with his rash decision.

Naomi walked into the kitchen. She looked through the drawers. *Butter knives?* No, she didn't need those. *Forks?* She figured she could cause some damage with a fork, but she was tired of cutting Mario. *Spoons?* A spoon could be used to gouge an eye out, but she had already damaged one of Mario's eyes. She grabbed a long, red grill lighter from one of the drawers. *Perfect,* she thought.

She returned to the living room and said, "Mario, you broke the rules. You know what that means, right? I have to punish you. I have to make sure you know who's boss."

With a smothered voice, Mario mumbled, "Pl– Please, don't do this. I–I'm begging you."

"It's either you or your daughter. Go ahead and

pick."

Mario looked down at his mutilated legs and sobbed. He felt a pins-and-needles sensation across his thighs, as if an army of insects were marching around his wounds. He still felt a stinging pain, too. He doubted his ability to endure more pain, but he wouldn't allow his daughter to take his punishment.

He mumbled, "Me... Hurt me..."

Naomi smirked and responded, "Good choice. And, don't worry, this one won't be as bad as the others. It's not as... elaborate, you know? I came up with it right off the top of my head. I think it's still going to hurt, though."

She stood behind Mario and pushed his head to his left. *Click, click, click*—she ignited the grill lighter. Mario was familiar with the sound. He thought: *what is she going to burn? My other eye? My bloody eye? My gums?* His thoughts were interrupted by the sudden heat near his right ear. The flame flickered an inch away from his ear lobe.

The vengeful woman leaned closer to his head and whispered, "You bit one of his ears off, so let me do something worse to you."

Mario's muffled pleas were not enough to stop her. Naomi shoved the barrel of the lighter into his right ear canal. The lighter remained ignited, too, burning his ear hair, ear wax, and eardrum. Mario shook on the chair, trying to pull away from the lighter to no avail. He heard a moist *crackling* sound in his ear and he felt a stinging, pulsating pain.

Naomi twirled her wrist and twisted the barrel in his ear. She shoved it as deep as possible without extinguishing the flame. Mario felt something *pop* in his ear, and that pop was accompanied by more pain. An incessant ringing sound quickly followed, then his ear felt full and warm—as if water had filled his ear during a dip in the pool. It wasn't water, though. A droplet of blood leaked out of his ear and streamed across his cheek.

Mario unleashed a bellow. Bouncing on his chair, he shook his head and cried. He let out all of his pain and sorrow, hoping someone—*somewhere*—would hear him.

Naomi pulled the lighter out of his ear. She whispered, "That was faster than I thought." She walked in front of his chair, then she leaned forward with her hands on her knees. She asked, "How does that feel? Can you hear me, Mario?"

Mario looked every which way. He tightly closed his eye, then he opened it, then he closed it again. He couldn't hear anything from his right ear and he couldn't see anything through his left eye. On the other hand, he could see from his right eye and hear from his left ear. It caused a jarring effect—up was down, left was right.

He thought: *what is she doing to me? What kind of sick game is this?* A frightening numbness set in on the side of his head. His breathing intensified as he instinctively panicked.

Snapping him out of his contemplation, Naomi said, "I won't mutilate your other eye or ear because I want you to see and hear the next steps of my plan. We can't talk if you can't hear. You can't witness true horror if you can't see." She stood straight and glanced around the living room. She said, "Let's get you two back to your places. We're not done talking yet."

Chapter Twelve

To Love a Monster

Naomi sat on the sofa and stared absently at the coffee table. She looked tired and distant, almost as if she didn't want to move forward with her own plan. She had already moved Mario and Vicky to their rightful places, so she took a moment to catch her breath.

Mario sat on his chair with his back to the kitchen while Vicky sat on her chair with her back to the patio doors. The couple were forced to face each other. Only the long coffee table separated them. Yet, to them, it felt like they were separated by miles and miles of desolation.

Mario was barely conscious. His injuries took a toll on him and he was exhausted. Vicky hadn't been tortured since the incident at the pool, though.

Naomi approached Vicky and said, "Same rules apply to you. If you scream, someone else dies. Maybe it'll be your husband, maybe it'll be your daughter. I don't know. I'll just flip a coin to decide. Do you understand me?" Eyes welling with tears, Vicky stared up at Naomi and nodded. Naomi said, "Good girl."

Naomi removed the tape from Vicky's mouth, allowing the strip to dangle down to her jaw. She sat down on the sofa at an angle, her legs facing Vicky. Vicky breathed deeply through her mouth, savoring each breath. She looked at Naomi, then she glanced over at Mario, then back at Naomi. Mario, weak and sluggish, was out of the picture at the moment.

Naomi said, "I'm sorry for neglecting you tonight. Since Mario is a little tired, I think now is a good time for us to talk. I know a lot about you and your family, but I don't know everything. Tell me how you two met. I'm curious."

Vicky asked, "Will you let us go if I tell you? Will you... Will you actually let us live if we cooperate?"

"Of course. I hurt you a little, but I didn't try to kill you, did I? I didn't hurt your daughter, either. Mario is a *little* injured, but he's not dead. Trust me, Vicky, I'm a woman of my word. So, how did you two meet? Come on, give me all of the juicy details."

Vicky stuttered, "We–Well, um... We met online."

"A dating site? Or maybe a dating app?" Naomi asked. She grinned and asked, "Did you 'swipe right,' Vicky? No, no. It couldn't have been an app. You met before all of that became popular, didn't you?"

As she stared at her husband, eyes glowing with hope, Vicky said, "Yeah, it wasn't an app or a dating site. We met on an internet forum. It was a forum for... for depressed people. We were both depressed for different reasons and we found some comfort in each other. We talked for months. I mean, we talked about everything: movies, music, books, dreams, depression. After a few months, we realized we lived in the same county. I thought that was why we felt so comfortable together. It felt like... like fate."

Naomi cocked her head to the side and pouted, as if to say: *aww, what a sweet story.* Mario stared at his wife, breathing noisily through his nose. The story warmed his broken heart. Tears streamed down

Vicky's cheeks with each blink as she gazed into her husband's good eye, trying her best to avoid the bloody eyepatch. She thought: *what has she done to you?*

Naomi said, "So, let me guess what happened next. You met in person, maybe at a bar or café, you chatted it up a bit, you fucked, you found out he slaughtered an innocent man, you fucked again, then you married him. And now you live happily ever after with the 'perfect' family. Is that right?"

Vicky said, "No, that's not how it happened. We met and we liked each other, but... after I found out he was *the* Mario Flores, we stopped talking. I said we needed a break, even though he explained that he was... *sick* back then."

Sick—Vicky said it with a pinch of uncertainty in her voice. She believed her husband was mentally unwell, but she knew Naomi didn't believe him. She didn't want to upset her.

Vicky continued, "The videos and pictures he sent me, the voicemails he left... I couldn't stand seeing him and I didn't want to listen to his voice anymore. He tried to contact me, but I just couldn't talk to him. I was scared of him and myself. I believed everything people like you said about him. 'He's a monster,' 'he's a psychopath,' and 'he'll do it again.' So, I just ran away from it all."

Naomi responded, "Interesting. So, what made you change your mind?"

Staring down at her lap, Vicky said, "I remembered something. The second time we met in person, Mario and I found an injured dog on the road. His leg was broken, his snout was cut, and his skin was irritated... He looked like he went through hell and no one stopped to help him, except for Mario. Mario did everything in his power to take care of that poor dog. He made sure that dog felt safe and comfortable during his time of need." She looked Naomi in the eye and said, "Mario killed Trevor, but he only did it because he was sick. It's unfortunate, it's tragic, but it's true. I don't believe a man who loves animals could ever *consciously* commit such a horrible crime. It's just not possible. Please, you have to believe us."

Naomi tilted her head to the side and furrowed her brow. She thought about Vicky's explanation. There were some facts behind her logic. Compared to the average person, psychopaths and sociopaths were more likely to intentionally torture animals. Sociopathy wasn't a strong legal defense, either. In fact, it couldn't be effectively used as part of an insanity plea.

For Mario to be found not guilty for reasons of insanity, he had to be diagnosed with something else —with a legitimate, court-approved mental illness. Naomi couldn't easily accept that fact.

Naomi said, "I think you got played, Vicky. You're telling me Mario's *not* insane, but he was found not guilty because they believed he was insane. It's–"

"He's not insane, he's sick."

"Don't interrupt me again or I'll cut your tongue out, you bitch."

Vicky closed her mouth and pulled her head back, backing down from the confrontation. She believed Naomi would actually sever her tongue.

Naomi said, "As I was saying, it's possible that

Mario saved that dog just to get into your pants, isn't it? Then, he probably took it home and killed it. Hell, he probably ate the poor thing. We both know he has some 'unnatural' tastes."

"No, that didn't happen. He adopted the dog and he was still alive when we got back together. He lived with us, *here,* until he died two years ago. Mario never lay a finger on him. He... He even shed tears for him when he passed away. He's not the monster you think he is."

Naomi narrowed her eyes and cocked her head back, surprised by the revelation. She glanced over at Mario. To her utter surprise, Mario already stared back at her. *You're a monster, aren't you?*–she thought.

Naomi sighed, then she said, "That's a nice story, Vicky. If it weren't for the murder, it would have been like a fairy tale—a troubled princess falls in love with a troubled man. My story was kind of like that, too, until the... the murder. You see, I had no luck in high school. Nope, I didn't get a high school sweetheart or anything like that. College? Shit, college was even worse. One day, you're in love. The next, Chad went and slept with your best friend. Now, I didn't actually date a Chad, but you get what I mean. I went through a bad breakup in college and that led to me failing most of my classes and *that* led to me dropping out of school. What do you think happened next?"

Vicky tried to shrug, but the tape around her body restricted her movement. She said, "I don't know. I guess you... you met Trevor."

"Yeah, eventually. But, before that, I worked

several little jobs. I was a cashier, a waitress, a maid... You get it. While I was working all of those jobs, I kept on thinking: my life is over. I figured I would have to settle for anyone. It's not like I expected Prince Charming or anything like that, but... you know, you kind of wish for the best for yourself, right? Eventually, I ended up meeting Trevor at a bar. He was there for a drink after work and I was there as a bartender. It was love at first sight. It really was."

Naomi smiled and tears filled her eyes. She looked up at the ceiling and reminisced about the past. Throughout the years—those cold, lonesome years—she never forgot Trevor's image. In her dreams, he resembled the same man she met at the bar. In her nightmares, she remembered the blood-soaked, stab-riddled, mutilated body from the bus.

Her voice shaking, she said, "When we met, he worked as a house painter. It wasn't a 'special,' high-paying job, but it was good. It was perfect. I imagined us painting our first house together. Hell, it didn't even have to be a house. I was happy to paint a room in our apartment with him. I found comfort in him, just like you found comfort in Mario. But, Trevor never did anything wrong. He never killed or hurt anyone..."

The glimmer in her eyes—a glimmer of hope and happiness—vanished. The memories cured her aching heart, but only for a moment. As she neared the end of her story, a jolt of emotional pain surged through her body.

In an unusually monotonous tone, Naomi said, "We went on the most romantic dates. There was one where Trevor fell off a boat because of one of my 'innocent' pranks and one where I fell off a small bridge because Trevor wanted payback. We spent one night singing one-hit wonders from the nineties at a karaoke bar. There were more, but... those dates are fading away. Fifteen years is a long time, isn't it?"

Vicky wanted to apologize for Mario's actions, but she knew the effort would be fruitless. *'Sorry' can't change the past, 'sorry' can't resurrect the dead,* she thought. If Mario could speak, he would have offered to kill himself in exchange for Naomi's peace of mind. The tape—a mere strip of duct tape—muted him like a television, though.

Her voice rising with anger, Naomi said, "The future was supposed to be special for us. We were doing everything right. Trevor had a good job, we rented a nice little house, our baby girl was healthy. Life was good and it was only going to get better. Trevor told me that and I believed him. It was supposed to be the perfect fairy tale. Then, Mario showed up and ruined everything." She wiped the tears from her eyes and glared at Mario. She said, "If you had killed anyone else's husband, this probably wouldn't be happening to you now. It's crazy how things work out, huh? It's like we were meant for... for *this.*"

108

Chapter Thirteen

The Decision

Naomi approached Mario's chair. Her fingertips on his moist brow, she pushed his head back and examined his good eye. *Still responsive,* she thought, *he's ready.* She pulled the tape off his mouth. As expected, Mario gasped for air as soon as the tape reached the center of his lips. His deep breaths were ragged and loud.

Naomi neatly folded the wrinkled tape on his cheek, then she gently slapped him. Mario muttered incoherently and shook his head, trying to dodge Naomi's hand.

Naomi said, "It's time for us to play a little game."

As Naomi walked back to the sofa and riffled through the bag, Mario stared down at himself and examined his legs. Despite the stitches, he could still see *into* the gashes on his thighs. He spotted a sparkling shard of glass in his flesh. The pain dwindled, replaced with a numb sensation. Crying, he thought: *will they have to amputate them? Can they fix my eye? What would I look like?*

He thought about his daughter. He wondered if Layla would still recognize him in the morning. He wondered if he would still be able to play with her in the future. He pictured himself on a wheelchair, rolling around with Layla at a park. He would be grateful to be alive, but he didn't know if Layla would still love him.

He looked over at Naomi and thought: *she made me into a monster, she did this on purpose.* He thought about the next step in her plan and, even without knowing a thing, he trembled in fear.

With a weak, cracking voice, Mario stuttered, "I– I'll do anything if you... if you just end it."

Naomi stopped riffling through the backpack. She glanced back at Mario and asked, "What?"

"Kill me. Go ahead and kill me. Just... Just leave my wife and my daughter out of this. They didn't do anything to deserve any of this. If you're going to... to kill me, just let them go and do it already. I don't want them to see me like this."

"Really? Why?"

Mario looked at his wife with a heavy-lidded eye. Vicky frowned and shook her head, as if to say: *don't be a hero, we can still get out of this.*

Mario said, "This is... too much. If my little Layla saw me like this, she would have nightmares for the rest of her life. You've scarred my wife enough already. You've... You've almost killed me. What's the point in keeping me alive like this? This is wrong. Please, ma'am, just let them go and kill me."

Naomi took her hands out of the bag and turned around. With her hands on her hips, she scowled at Mario. The hatred in her eyes resurfaced. The trip down memory lane was over and it was time to handle business.

She said, "I identified Trevor that day. Sure, I could have taken the easy way and let the police handle it, but I had to see him. I couldn't tell myself that I truly loved him if I just ran away. He was dead, but I couldn't leave him alone in his time of need. So, you see, I *had* to see him. That means you have to witness your family's pain, too." She looked over at Vicky and said, "And you have to see your husband's suffering. That's it."

Naomi returned to the bag, breathing deeply through her nose. An image of Trevor's mutilated body flashed in her mind when she mentioned him. She was hurt by the memory, so tears flooded her eyes. Yet, despite her blurred vision, she still found herself searching for her next tool. She was determined to exact her revenge.

As Naomi searched, Vicky said, "I won't beg you to release me. I understand your anger and your pain. I just hope that you can find it in your heart to release Layla. She's innocent in all of this. Punish me, punish Mario, but please spare our child. Show us that you're not the monster you set out to kill."

Naomi said, "We'll get to that when the time comes." She stopped looking through the backpack. Her hands still in the bag, she said, "It's time to play."

She pulled both of her hands out of the bag at the same time. In her left hand, she held a slotted screwdriver. In her right hand, she held a black, hammer-less .357 revolver. Both weapons were equally terrifying.

Mario cried, "No, no, no. No, goddammit! You can't do this! It's not right!"

"Stop screaming," Naomi demanded.

Practically hyperventilating, Vicky stammered, "You–You–You have to–to let her go. Please, do–don't kill my baby! Don't do this!"

"Be quiet!" Naomi shouted. She aimed the gun at the ceiling and said, "If you keep screaming, I'm going to go upstairs to blow your daughter's brains out. You understand me, you dumb fucks? Do you understand me?!"

The couple became quiet in an instant. Vicky sucked her lips inward and shook her head, fighting the urge to scream. Mario bit his bottom lip and whimpered, broken breaths escaping his nose.

Naomi turned her attention to Mario and said, "It's time to make a decision. It's going to be a tough one, but you have to make it. If you don't, things will get worse for everyone."

Mario asked, "What do you want from me?"

"I want you to pick one," Naomi said coldly. She leaned forward and gazed into his eye. She asked, "Do you want me to kill your wife or your daughter?"

Mario's eye widened upon hearing the question. He was willing to die for his crime. He offered his life to Naomi. Instead, she flipped the tables on him and threatened to murder someone he loved. *Cold-hearted bitch,* he thought, *you're the monster, not me.* Of course, he didn't dare insult her. She had a gun after all.

Mario stuttered, "Wha–What? I–I thought... I thought this was about vengeance. I thought it was an–an eye for an eye. I never forced you to make a decision like this."

Naomi said, "You're right. You didn't give us any options. You just took what you wanted. So, you really should be thanking me, Mario. I'm giving you an opportunity here. You can mold the future, you can choose to save someone. Now, do you want me to kill Vicky or Layla with the gun? Come on, pick one."

"I can't."

"You can. You're a grown man. You can make a decision."

"No, please don't do this."

Naomi exhaled loudly, then she said, "Okay, let's try it this way. Just tell me which one you love the least. Can you do that for me?"

Saliva dripping from his mouth, Mario shook his head and cried, "I can't do it. I love them both so much. They–They're everything to me. Don't make me do this. I'm begging you."

Vicky sniffled and said, "Kill me. If it's between me and my baby girl, just kill me. I–I'm okay with it."

Naomi asked, "Did you hear that, Mario? Vicky wants to die. Should I do it?"

"Yes," Vicky cried. "Oh, God, yes! Just do it already!"

"No, not yet. Mario has to give me the word."

Mario lowered his head and sobbed. His saliva dripped onto his thighs, but he didn't feel it. He was overwhelmed by the pressure. He thought about the years he spent with Vicky, then an image of Layla flashed in his mind. Their overlapping voices echoed through his head. He gritted his teeth and grunted as he tried to bounce on his chair. He thought: *she's doing this on purpose, that bitch, she wants me to be responsible for their deaths.*

He yelled, "I can't decide! I love both of them! I fucking love them!"

Naomi said, "Love can't save them."

Mario grunted and bounced on his seat again, frustrated. His eye widened as an idea formed in his head. *I can still save them,* he thought, *I just need to give her what she wants.*

His eye glimmering with hope, he looked at Naomi and said, "I faked it. Okay? It was... It was all fake. I'm not sick! I faked everything!"

Naomi said, "Oh, *really?*" She huffed and smiled, skeptical but interested. She said, "Okay. So, what did you say that made them believe you were crazy? How did you convince all of those doctors? Hmm? Or did you pay someone off? Tell me your story, Mario. I'm listening."

"I... I just told them... I can't remember what I said."

"You can't remember? Or you can't think of something off the top of your head?"

"No, no. I... I told them whatever came to mind. You know, I told them stuff from movies and books. I was just a–a cliché 'crazy' person. I told them about the voice of God and shit like that."

Naomi stared at Mario with a deadpan expression. Mario stared back at her, trying to keep an expression of sincerity on his face—straight lips, a steady nose, a hopeful eye. *Please believe me,* he thought, *don't hurt my family, just let us go.*

Naomi chuckled and shook her head—amused, amazed, *annoyed.* She said, "That's the type of bullshit I expected from a liar like you."

"I'm not lying. I'm not sick. I'm just a... a psycho, like you said."

"You were either lying to me at the beginning of the night or you're lying to me now. Either way, you're a liar. I can't trust you."

Naomi walked around the sofa, taking slow,

steady steps. She headed for the stairs, but she took her time. She wanted to build the tension in the room in order to torment her captives. It was fun to her.

As she took her stroll, weapons clenched in her hands, she said, "If you don't choose, I'm going to go upstairs to murder your daughter. Then, I'll come back down here and kill Vicky. Okay? As soon as I step on that first stair, your time is up."

Mario cried, "No! No, damn it! Please don't do this! I'm begging you, miss. I'll pay you, I'll kill myself, I'll do anything."

Naomi took one step, then another, and then another. She said, "You can still choose."

"I can't! Why won't you listen to me? Why?!"

Naomi took two more steps—two slow, dreadful strides. She stood no more than a meter away from the foot of the stairs.

Vicky shouted, "Kill me!"

"He has to choose," Naomi said.

Vicky glanced over at Mario and, in a fast, panicky voice, she said, "Tell her to kill me. It's okay, honey. I love you. I'll love you no matter what. Just save Layla! Tell her to kill me already!"

Mario grimaced upon hearing the sound of another creaky footsteps. The shrill creak drilled into his only good ear. *I'm out of time,* he thought, *she won, I can't save both of them.*

Mario closed his eye and shouted, "Vicky! I choose Vicky!"

Naomi stopped at the foot of the stairs. She said, "As you wish, Mario."

***

As Naomi walked back to Vicky's chair, Mario said, "Vicky, sweetheart, I'm so sorry. I never wanted any of this to happen. I just... I wanted to be happy with you. I wanted us to live a good life. I love you so much, sweetie. I love you."

"I love you, too," Vicky responded as she sniffled.

Stony-faced, Naomi aimed the revolver at Vicky. Mario closed his eye and turned away, refusing to witness his wife's inevitable death.

Naomi said, "Open your eyes... Sorry, open your *eye* and watch. Witness the consequences of your actions, you coward." Mario clenched his jaw and shook his head, defiant like a child. Naomi said, "If you don't watch your wife's death, I'll shoot Layla, too."

Mario glared at Naomi and barked, "Goddamn you, you fucking cunt!"

As she stared at Mario, a cold look in her eyes, Naomi pulled the trigger. Mario flinched upon hearing the booming gunfire. The gunshot echoed through the home and even seeped out of the house. Layla heard the gunshot from her bedroom, but she didn't recognize the sound. She only knew it wasn't good.

Vicky stared down at her right leg. She was shot in her thigh. The bullet was lodged in her flesh. She initially felt a strong pinch, then she felt a pricking sensation, and then the pain increased. Her thigh burned with a sharp stinging pain. The mere sight of the warm blood oozing out of the wound somehow worsened the pain, too.

She panted and sobbed. She tried to rock back and forth in her seat. The tape around her torso stopped her, though, so she only moved her head back-and-forth—like a bobblehead.

Naomi asked, "It hurts, doesn't it?"

Vicky couldn't conjure the words to respond. The insufferable pain temporarily wiped her vocabulary.

Mario said, "Vicky, look at me, hun. It's almost over. I swear, it's almost over. Just stay strong, baby. I'm going to take care of everything. Don't... Don't be scared."

"It hurts!" Vicky cried, agony laced in her voice.

"I know it hurts, sweetheart. You just have to–"

Mid-sentence, Naomi shot Vicky again. The bullet smashed through her upper abdomen and penetrated her stomach. Vicky immediately stopped crying. Veins protruded from her brow and her face reddened as she held her breath. The gunshot felt like an uppercut from a heavyweight boxer. It knocked the air out of her and nearly knocked her unconscious. A stinging pain followed, as if acid were being poured into the wound. The pain was unbearable.

His teeth chattering, Mario asked, "Wha–What are you doing to her? Why... Why are you torturing her like this? She didn't do anything to you."

Vicky coughed and groaned as she struggled to breathe. She felt nauseous and dizzy. A cold sweat drenched her body, soaking her nightgown.

Naomi crouched down next to Vicky's chair and placed the revolver on the floor. She shoved her index fingers through the bullet hole on her nightgown, then she separated her fingers and ripped the garment. Vicky's firm stomach, stained with a streak of blood, was revealed through the wide gap on her nightgown. Blood dribbled out of the gunshot wound, streaming down to her belly button.

Mario watched Naomi, his eyelids twitching due to his anxiety and fear. He wanted to comfort his wife, but it seemed hopeless. Vicky couldn't soothe his pain during his torture, so he knew he couldn't soothe hers. He couldn't stop Naomi, either.

He said, "I love you, Vicky. I hope you can... forgive me for this. This is all my fault. Damn it, I'm sorry." He grimaced as Naomi raised the screwdriver. Tears and blood streaming down his cheeks, he said, "Don't do it. Don't do it, ma'am..."

Naomi forced the tip of the screwdriver into the gunshot wound on Vicky's abdomen. Vicky shrieked in pain and her body involuntarily jerked every which way. Tightly gripping the handle, Naomi twisted her wrist and forced the screwdriver into the wound, drilling it as deep as possible. A geyser of blood squirted out, splattering on her face and raincoat.

Vicky's eyelids flickered and her lips quivered as Naomi thrust the screwdriver in and out of her wound. The pain increased with each thrust, reverberating across her entire body. Mario noticed the pain on Vicky's scrunched up face. He spotted the suffering in her hollow eyes. Yet, Naomi wouldn't stop aggravating the wound with the screwdriver.

Mario shouted, "Stop it! Damn it, stop!"

Naomi pulled the screwdriver out of Vicky's abdomen, which caused more blood to jet out, then she tossed it on the coffee table. She grabbed the revolver and stood up, swiping at the blood on her face. Vicky panted and convulsed, blood and saliva foaming from her mouth. Naomi aimed the gun at Vicky's head, the muzzle floating an inch away from her right temple.

She asked, "When should I finish her, Mario? Hmm? I'll let you choose. Just say the words: 'kill my beloved wife.' Then, I'll end her suffering. If you can't say the words, I'll just keep playing with her. So, what will it be? You ready to end it?"

Mario's face became paler than ever before. *She's hurting her, but she's still torturing me,* he thought. He realized Naomi was psychologically toying with him. She truly wanted him to bear the responsibility of Vicky's death. Vicky nodded at her husband, as if to say: *say it, kill me.* She looked weak and horrified, hollow-eyed and shaking.

Mario weakly said, "Do it..."

"Say the words," Naomi demanded.

"Damn it," Mario muttered. He stared at Vicky, eye glistening with tears, and he said, "Kill my beloved wife."

"Good."

Naomi placed the muzzle of the revolver on Vicky's temple. Vicky flinched and cried upon feeling the gun. She closed her eyes and waited for her inevitable death to arrive. To her dismay, Naomi didn't pull the trigger. The intruder purposely waited in order to psychologically torture her as well.

Naomi asked, "What happens when you die, Vicky? Is heaven waiting for you on the other side? Or does it all fade to black? Does it fade to... nothingness? Will you even know any of this happened? What do you think death feels like? Hmm?"

Realizing what she was doing, Mario cried out, "Stop it! Leave her alone! Don't... Don't hurt her like this. She doesn't deserve this!"

In a soft voice, Vicky stuttered, "I–I don't know... I don't know what happens."

Naomi responded, "I wish I did. It's scary, isn't it? You're going to die soon and you don't know what's coming."

Mario barked, "Kill my beloved wife! Kill her! Just do it al–"

Naomi pulled the trigger, interrupting him with the loud gunfire. Vicky's head swung to the left, then her head fell to her chest. It was a through-and-through shot—in on one side, out through the other. A streak of dark blood and pink brains painted the floor and wall with every tint of red. Blood leaked from both sides of her head.

Mario could only sit and stare at Vicky's pale face. He was rendered speechless by her sudden death. He knew it was coming, but he wasn't ready for it. He thought: *this can't be happening, she's actually dead.* A torrent of memories flooded his mind. He remembered all of their online chats, their first date, their last date, Layla's birth, and their last phone call —*everything.*

Naomi and Mario stayed quiet for a minute. Only the sound of blood *plopping* on the floor emerged in the room—*drip, drip, drip.*

Naomi lowered the gun and said, "I'm going to leave Vicky in her seat until this is over. You deserve to see her like this. It'll make you feel more pain. The same pain I felt when I saw Trevor's corpse, the same pain I *feel* whenever I think of Trevor."

Mario remained speechless. His mind was addled by his wife's death, limiting his ability to think clearly. Naomi sat down on the sofa and aimed the revolver at Mario's stomach. She just killed someone, but she didn't seem bothered by her own actions. She looked colder than usual.

Naomi said, "I'll give you a few minutes to gather your thoughts and calm down. I know what it's like to lose a spouse." She glanced over at Vicky and said, "You made the wrong choice, Mario. I know it looked bad, but Vicky got out the easy way."

Mario glared at Naomi. He thought: *what is that supposed to mean? Is she threatening my daughter? Is she going to hurt Layla?* Her deception infuriated him, but he still couldn't say a word. He waited for the next step in her diabolical plan.

Chapter Fourteen

Feelings

"How do you feel, Mario?" Naomi asked, still aiming the revolver at her captive.

Mario was insulted by the question. He was confused, depressed, and angry. He wanted to respond by saying something along the lines of: *how did you feel when I killed Trevor?* He didn't want to jeopardize his daughter's safety, though. So, he bit his tongue, he looked at his dead wife, and he trembled with rage.

Naomi said, "Your hands and your feet have been broken. You might never move your toes or fingers again. Your legs... Damn it, look at what I did to your legs. Your thighs have been mangled. I tried to stitch those cuts, but... They were deep, Mario—*real deep.* With the glass shards and the lemon, I think you might get an infection. They might have to amputate your legs. They'll have to cut 'em off. Chop, chop..."

She stared at his face and waited for his reaction —hostile or forgiving—but he didn't respond to her. Mario kept his eyes on his wife, fighting to keep his composure. He heard all of her words, though. He understood her game.

Naomi said, "Your eye... Your poor eye... You'll never see from that eye again. They'll give you a prosthetic, it might move with your other eye, it might *look* like your other eye, but you'll *never* see from it again. I fucked with your hearing, too, didn't

I? I don't know much about that. Can they repair it? We'll probably never know. So... how does all of that make you feel?"

Mario slowly turned towards Naomi. He screamed at the top of his lungs. His shout grew louder as his mouth widened—inch-by-inch. He bounced on his chair, trying his best to move forward and lunge at his captor. Like a feral animal with rabies, saliva foamed out of his mouth and dripped onto his boxers.

The volume of the shout dwindled as he ran out of breath, then he stopped screaming. He breathed heavily and glared at Naomi. Words of hatred were clogged in his throat: bitch, whore, motherfucker, slut, cunt.

Naomi said, "I know how you feel. You're going through the... the stages of grief. When I killed her, you probably thought: this can't be happening. No, you thought: this *isn't* happening. That's what you thought while I was murdering your wife, right? That's denial, Mario. That's the first stage."

Mario continued to breathe deeply. He listened to her words while thinking about murder. *Bite her neck,* he thought, *bite her face off.*

Naomi said, "The next stage is anger, which is what you're probably experiencing now. I don't have to explain anger to you, do I?"

"Fuck you," Mario hissed through his gritted teeth.

"I thought so. After your fit of anger, you'll want to bargain. I'm not talking about making a deal with me, though. No, you're going to wish it was you instead of her. You're going to wish you could magically go back in time and stop yourself from killing Trevor in order to save Vicky. But, of course, none of that is going to happen because they're dead. Vicky is dead. Can you say that? Hmm? Can you?"

His voice shaking, Mario said, "I'm going to kill you."

Disregarding the threat, Naomi continued, "When you finally come to terms with her death, you'll go into a 'depressive state.' That's what my doctor called it. It's just depression. And, like a disease, depression will eat away at your body and your mind. It will feel like you're... you're decaying. It will make you want to give up, it will make you want to kill yourself. Depression is mankind's worst enemy. It's something that can invite itself into our minds, make itself at home, then kill us from within. It's fucked up."

Mario understood Naomi's pain. He realized that she was very familiar with the stages of grief because she had already fought through the cycle. Still, he couldn't sympathize with his wife's killer. He thought: *you can kill without remorse, you're not afraid of my threats and you're not afraid of the law, you are mankind's worst enemy.*

Staring absently at the coffee table, Naomi said, "If you survive the depression, you'll reach the stage of acceptance. That sounds great, doesn't it? It sounds peaceful, right? What they don't tell you is: everything won't be okay. You're not accepting a 'happy' new life, you're just accepting the fact that you can't change the past and you have to move on. It's bullshit, but that's the way it is. That's the way the world spins..."

Silence befell the room—*dead silence.* The wounds on Vicky's head finally stopped dripping. Mario's breathing became slow and relaxed, and Naomi's breathing was barely negligible. They didn't hear a peep from upstairs, either.

Breaking the silence, Naomi glanced over at Mario and said, "No one talks about it, doctors definitely won't mention it, but there is a sixth stage of grief. It's called vengeance. It's the next logical step for victims like us." She leaned forward, her elbows on her knees. She narrowed her eyes and said, "If you weren't tied up, you would be trying to kill me right now. You'd move quickly through the stages of grief, you'd murder me, then it would all start again. You would love to avenge your wife right now, wouldn't you?"

With a raspy voice, Mario said, "I want... to... kill you. You don't... You don't deserve to live. You're the evil one, not me. You..." He chuckled deliriously. He said, "You shouldn't have washed those pills down the drain 'cause you need 'em more than me."

Naomi wasn't amused. She watched Mario, eyes as narrow as a pair of blades. She looked at him as if she were analyzing him, breaking down his psyche.

She said, "After Trevor died, I experienced... shock. You know what I mean? I was just hit with everything. I was diagnosed with post-traumatic stress disorder and depression. I had never-ending thoughts of suicide. To this day, I can't even look at a damn bus without having a panic attack! I can't do it, Mario, and it's because of what you did!"

She breathed loudly through her nose and tried

to recompose herself. She swiped at the tears clinging to her eyelids, but she didn't look away from him. She didn't have to worry about showing weakness around Mario anymore anyway. She already proved her willingness to commit heinous crimes through her acts of torture and murder.

She said, "What you're experiencing now, you forced that on dozens of people. Yeah, don't forget about the people who were actually *on* the bus when you attacked Trevor. There were teenagers on that bus! Kids, Mario, *kids!* And they can't live normal lives, either. You scarred all of them with your actions. Did you know that? Does it even bother you to know that now?"

Mario didn't respond. Truth be told, he rarely thought about the other passengers on the bus. He apologized to the bus driver, but he forgot about the others. *I'm selfish,* he thought, *but that doesn't make me a monster like her.*

Naomi nodded and said, "I spent a lot of time with them. We even had several group therapy sessions to talk about that horrible day. It's one thing to be an 'edgy' kid who watches people die on the internet, it's a whole 'nother thing to actually experience it. People aren't supposed to see things like that. No, we're supposed to be safe, aren't we? We're supposed to be in a bubble, right? That's what we think until someone shows up and pops that bubble. You popped ours, so I'm here to pop yours..."

Mario sighed, then he asked, "Are you done?"

"What?"

"Are you finished? Is it over? You... You killed Vicky. You tortured me. I think we're even now. So, kill me, cover our bodies, let my daughter go, and... and leave. Kill me so I can finally pay for my crimes, so we can finally end this."

Naomi clicked her tongue and shook her head. She said, "I'm sorry to break it to you, Mario, but we're not done yet. You killed my husband and ruined my life. You've been torturing me for fifteen years, you just didn't know it. Plus, you've been lying to me all night. There's no way I can let this night end without a bang." She stood from her seat and said, "We have to work fast, though. We don't have much time now. The police will be here soon. Someone probably heard those gunshots, right?"

Chapter Fifteen

Daughters

Naomi tugged on the curtain dangling over the patio doors. The curtain rod above the doors detached from the wall with a *clunking* sound. With that, she was able to easily remove the curtain from the pole. She threw the curtain over Vicky's body, covering the wounds on her head, torso, and thigh. Her bloody leg was still visible, but there was nothing she could do about it.

Baffled, Mario stuttered, "Wha–What are you doing?"

As she organized the curtain, ensuring it wouldn't fall off the dead body, Naomi said, "You deserve to see her like this, Mario, but she doesn't."

"Who doesn't?"

Naomi casually strolled across the living room. Mario could see she was heading for the stairs. There was nothing for her upstairs—except Layla.

His eye locked on her, Mario asked, "Where are you going? What are you doing?" Naomi ignored his questions and walked up the stairs. Mario barked, "Stop! Don't do it! I'm right here! Kill me, damn it!"

Naomi stopped at the top of the stairs, her eyes glued to the first door to her left. She closed her eyes and took a deep breath. Mario's screaming dwindled until his voice completely vanished. She thought: *there's no turning back from this.*

She opened her eyes and whispered, "I'm sorry,

sweetie."

Naomi quietly entered Layla's bedroom. She was surprised to see Layla slumbering in her bed. She wondered if the girl even heard the gunshots and the screaming or if she had just fallen asleep. *Does she know her mother is dead?*–she thought. She sat on the edge of the bed and caressed Layla's cheek.

Layla's eyes opened to a tired squint. Her eyes widened with fear upon recognizing Naomi. She was pulled out of a sweet dream and dropped into a horrific nightmare.

As she stroked Layla's hair, Naomi said, "Hey, hun. I'm sorry about leaving you earlier without explaining everything. I'm sorry if you, um... if you heard all of the noise downstairs. I'm sorry for... for what I'm going to do." She breathed shakily and tears dripped from her eyes. She swallowed the lump in her throat, then she said, "Just remember, sweetie, you have to be brave. No matter what, you have to stay strong. The more you cry, the more you hurt your daddy. Stay strong, hun."

Layla didn't understand the situation, but she knew her family was in danger. *How am I going to hurt daddy if I cry?*–she thought. She was frightened by Naomi's words, she felt threatened by the tone of her voice. She squirmed on the bed, hopelessly trying to escape. She was able to shuffle to the other side of the mattress.

As her tears dripped on the bed sheets, Naomi pulled a switchblade out of her pocket and cut the rope that tied Layla to the bedposts. She didn't cut the rope around her wrists and ankles, though. One arm under her legs and the other supporting her back, she lifted Layla's flailing body from the bed and walked out of the bedroom.

As Layla wiggled in her arms, Naomi leaned closer to her ear and whispered, "Remember what I said: it will all be over soon. Don't cry, baby."

She carried Layla down the stairs. The sound of each creaky step sounded louder than ever before because of their combined weight.

Mario recognized the sound. He had carried Layla to her bedroom dozens of times. It was the same sound—the same damn sound. His eye widened as soon as he spotted Layla in Naomi's arms. A mixture of anger, fear, and sadness surged through his body. His thoughts were jumbled, so he couldn't say a word.

He felt a sharp pain in his only good ear upon hearing his daughter's whimpers. As soon as he locked eyes with Layla, his heart shattered. He thought: *I'm sorry, sweetie-pie, I failed you as a parent.*

As Naomi reached the bottom of the stairs, Mario stuttered, "Wha–Wha–What are you doing? You–You can't do this. I made the decision! We... We had a deal! Let her go!"

Naomi kicked a door open in the dining area to the left of the living room. The door led to a small but full bathroom—it had a toilet, a sink, a medicine cabinet, and a bathtub and shower combination. Balancing Layla's squirming body in her arms, she flicked the light switch with her elbow, then she stepped into the room.

She placed Layla in the bathtub and said, "Don't move, Layla. If you get up, I'm going to hurt your parents."

Although her voice was muffled, Layla said something along the lines of: *I'm scared, please let me go.* She could see Naomi's threat was genuine, though. So, she reluctantly nodded in agreement. She continued to wiggle and slide in the bathtub, but she couldn't stand up.

As Naomi walked into the living room, Mario said, "You can't do this to us. I played your game, I followed your rules! I made the decision, didn't I? I did what you asked me to do, didn't I?"

Ignoring his words, Naomi grabbed the backrest of Mario's chair. She took a deep breath, then she dragged him across the room. A screeching sound echoed through the house as the chair's legs scratched the floorboards. She positioned him three meters away from the bathroom door, giving him the perfect view of the bathtub—and his daughter.

Naomi rubbed his shoulders and said, "It'll be over soon."

***

Layla squirmed in the bathtub, slipping and sliding on the smooth surface. She placed her chin on the edge of the tub and stared out the bathroom. She grimaced and shuddered in fear upon spotting her father. She was frightened by his appearance—his bloodied face and ear, his broken hands and feet, his sliced thighs, and even his eyepatch.

She whimpered and fell back into the bathtub. She thought: *it's just a scary dream, monsters aren't real.*

Mario shouted, "Layla! Layla, sweetie, everything's going to be okay. I'm here, baby! I'm still here! It's... It's me, your... your daddy. Please don't be scared, baby. Please..." He started crying, wheezing, and coughing. He shook his head and whispered, "I'm so sorry, baby. This wasn't supposed to happen to you."

During the family reunion, Naomi crouched down behind the recliner. She hid other supplies in the shadow of the chair before Mario arrived. Mario looked over at her, equally curious and horrified. He muttered incoherently to himself as she emerged from behind the recliner with a red jerrycan of gasoline and a small fire extinguisher. She carried the supplies to the bathroom.

Mario asked, "What are you doing? What are you planning?" Naomi unlocked the spout on the gas can. Mario cried, "No, no, no. Don't do this. I'm begging you. I'm fucking begging you, goddammit! Please, stop this and talk to me!"

Naomi ignored Mario's pleas. She approached the bathtub, gasoline can in hand. She stared down at the girl and watched her struggle. Then, she dumped the gasoline on her body. Some of the fluid splattered on the walls, the rest of it landed in the tub. The girl's muffled cry seeped past the tape as the gasoline dripped into her eyes.

Naomi dumped nearly eight liters of gasoline into the bathtub. Most of it swirled down the drain, but she was able to soak Layla's pajamas.

As he sobbed, Mario shouted, "Don't! You bitch! You sick cunt! You... You fucking monster! Don't do it! Don't hurt her! I swear, you'll regret it! I will never forgive you, I will *never* let this go! If I survive, I'll... I'll come after you! I'll make you feel *real* suffering! Damn it, don't do this!"

Naomi whispered, "Layla, it's almost over. You'll see your mother soon, okay? Stay strong, hun."

Layla heard Naomi's words of reassurance. The pain from her stinging eyes distorted her thoughts, though. Mario could hear Naomi's voice, but he didn't hear her words over his screaming. For all he knew, she could have been trying to scare her.

Mario said, "Layla, get up, baby. Get up and get out. Layla... Layla, look at me, sweetheart. You can do this. Get out of there and run."

Layla, wrists and ankles bound, thrashed about until she could peek over the edge of the bathtub again. Her vision was blurred by the gasoline, but she could still see her father and Naomi. She couldn't help but cry. Her father looked monstrous in her eyes, bloody and warped. She thought: *is he really a monster like she said?*

She shook her head, trying to shrug off the disturbing thoughts. She couldn't abandon her father, just like he couldn't abandon her.

Her voice muffled by the tape, Layla said: *daddy, I love you.*

Mario glared at Naomi and said, "Hey, look at me. Mrs. Morrison, please look at me." Naomi walked up to the doorway. Mario said, "I don't... I don't know what to say to convince you, but I *truly* lied about everything. I never heard voices in my head. The only voice in my head was my own—my sick, perverted voice. I killed Trevor because... because I felt like it. I was obsessed with murder and I just had to kill someone. Your husband was the perfect target —nice, skinny, oblivious. Shit, I was never sick and I never took that damn medicine. I just flushed it down the toilet every night. I've been living a lie and I deserve to be punished. Let my girl go and... and do your worse to me. Cut my stomach open and–and shove a rat in there. Open my thighs again, stick some... some feces in those gashes, then stitch me up again. Torture me. I deserve it."

Naomi stared at Mario with a steady expression as she leaned on the doorway. *You're lying again, aren't you?*–she thought. From the fear in his voice, she could tell he really didn't want to be tortured. However, she admired his willingness to sacrifice himself. He loved his daughter—that wasn't a lie.

Naomi said, "You're one sick man, Mario. Put feces in your cuts? What the hell is up with that?"

"I'm sorry, I just thought–"

"It doesn't matter anyway. I can't believe anything you say, so we'll never know the truth. You should have said something when the night started. It's too late now."

"No, no, no. Please don't say that. Please..."

Naomi pulled a matchbook out of her pocket. The matchbook was decorated with the image of a drunk cartoon peacock drinking from a mug of beer. The matchbook was labeled: *The Peacock's Beer & Lounge.* At that bar—not the fanciest place in the world—Naomi met and fell in love with Trevor.

Teary-eyed, Naomi wagged the matchbook at Mario and said, "There was something else I didn't tell you. There was another victim... a forgotten victim. My baby girl, Riley... She killed herself two years ago. She slit her... her wrists and hung... hung herself in her closet. She was only fourteen years old, almost fifteen... She was just a baby."

Mario was awed by the revelation. He understood Naomi's pain, the mere thought of losing his daughter broke his heart, but he didn't know how to respond. Apologies didn't help him, threats didn't persuade her to stop.

Naomi continued, "I blame myself. I was a bad mother, a *weak* mother. While I was seeking therapy for myself, trying to save myself from my worst nightmares, I didn't realize I was neglecting my only daughter. I... I tried to climb out of my depression while pushing my daughter into it. I ignored her pain, I missed the signs. I carry her coffin on my shoulders." She scowled at Mario and said, "And so do you. If Riley still had her father, if her family was never destroyed at such a young age, she wouldn't have died. If you didn't slaughter Trevor, I would still have my baby. If you never came into the picture, I would still be living in my own fairy tale."

Mario said, "I'm sorry. I'm—"

Naomi walked into the bathroom. She pulled the tape from Layla's mouth with one swift tug. Layla screamed and sobbed. Saliva dripped from her mouth as she mumbled incoherently about her parents. The girl only wanted to see her mother.

"Don't hurt her," Mario said. "Please, just... think of your daughter. Layla is innocent."

Naomi gently shushed Layla and caressed her hair, trying her best to comfort her. Layla was hysterical, though. She wouldn't stop crying until she was in her mother's arms.

In a gentle tone, Naomi said, "I'm sorry, hun. I'm so sorry. Mommy and Trevor and... and Riley are waiting for you in Heaven. It's almost over."

Layla cried, "Stop it! I want my mommy! Daddy, I want mommy!"

Mario shouted, "It's okay, baby! Daddy's here! You hear me? I'm still here!"

Naomi staggered to the center of the bathroom. She grimaced as she stared down at the horrified girl. *I can't stop,* she thought, *I have to do it.* Her fingers trembled as she plucked a match from the matchbook. She slid the match across the strike strip, igniting the thin piece of wood.

Upon noticing the flame, Mario yelled, "Don't! Please, I'm begging you! Oh, God, don't you–"

Mid-sentence, Naomi threw the match into the bathtub. A ball of fire immediately burst towards the ceiling. The fire crawled up the walls, ignited the bottles of shampoo and soap, and spread to the shower curtain within seconds. Plumes of smoke rose to the ceiling and undulated out of the room through the doorway.

The crackling flames swallowed every inch of Layla's small, pure body. Her milky skin reddened, wrinkled, and peeled. Blood oozed out from under her peeling skin, streaming across her body. Her hair sizzled and crackled while her scalp burned. Her eyes appeared to whiten, as if they had rolled to the back of her head.

Her pajamas blackened and ripped with the fire. Flakes of her burned skin and clothing floated through the air.

Fueled by his irrepressible rage and sadness, Mario shouted, "Layla! No, baby, no! I'm sorry, hun! I'm–"

He stopped shouting in order to sob and retch. His daughter's crying led to a massive headache and a broken heart. The stench of burning skin and hair meandered into his nostrils. The scent made him feel nauseous. His uselessness made him feel angrier than ever before.

He glared at Naomi and barked, "You fucking cunt! You goddamn cunt! You... You... Goddammit, Layla, I'm sorry. I love you, sweetheart! I love you so much!"

Layla, shrieking and weeping, writhed in pain in the bathtub. She tried to cry for her parents, but she couldn't form a single word. The pain was insufferable, surging across her whole body.

After forty-five seconds of burning, Layla rolled herself into the fetal position—her limbs locked in place. She stopped moving, she stopped breathing. Her skin became black, red, and even yellow. The fire had burned through all of her clothes and skin, roasting her muscles, tendons, and bones.

Mario watched in awe as Naomi put the fire out with the fire extinguisher. He just witnessed his daughter's brutal death. It felt surreal to him. The entire process lasted less than ten minutes, but he felt as if he had been sitting on that chair for ten years. *Layla's dead,* he thought, *she's killed everyone, except me.*

After extinguishing the fire, Naomi walked behind Mario's chair. She grabbed the backrest, then she pushed him forward.

Mario cried, "Why are you doing this? You don't–"

He stopped and whimpered as soon as he reached the bathroom doorway. He could see Layla's charred body in the bathtub.

His voice squeaky and shrill, he said, "God... God, no... How did... Why... I'm sorry, Layla."

Naomi sternly said, "Look at that girl, Mario. That's your daughter and she's dead because of you. If you really were guilty, you should have had some common decency and you should have killed yourself a long time ago. Instead, you built this fairy-tale life and put two innocent people in harm's way. You're as responsible for all of tonight's death as I am."

She closed the bathroom door, sealing Layla's dead body with a cloud of smoke. She grabbed the backrest of Mario's chair and dragged him back to the living room. She ignored his hopeless whimpering and muttering as she returned him to his regular position—directly across from his dead wife. She then walked over to Vicky and removed the curtain from over her body.

Naomi said, "Look at her, too, bastard. Look at her! This is all your fault!"

Mario sobbed hysterically, struggling to cope with the death of his family. His physical pain dwindled while his emotional suffering was amplified. He was absolutely devastated. He could only babble and groan.

Naomi said, "This isn't over, Mario. We still have time for one more experiment, for one more punishment..."

Chapter Sixteen

An Experiment

The acrid scent of burnt flesh meandered through the house—an unusually sweet but putrid stench. The scent of the smoke lingered in the house, too. The home was eerily quiet while the sound of purring engines emerged from outside. The neighborhood was finally starting to awaken. The early birds were heading to their worms.

Mario didn't have the energy to scream, though. He was physically and emotionally defeated. The stench of death and the dead silence tormented him. So, he just sat on his chair and sniffled as he thought about Vicky and Layla—as he thought about giving up. He reached the fourth stage of grief: *depression.*

Naomi pulled a cordless power drill out of the backpack. She squeezed the trigger, which caused the 19-millimeter drill bit to spin. The buzzing sound from the drill didn't seem to bother Mario. He stared vacantly at his dead wife, lost in his clouded, labyrinthine mind. He tried to escape his depression, but he kept running into dead-ends.

Snapping him out of his contemplation, Naomi said, "Mario, look at me. Are you listening?" Mario looked over at Naomi, his eye barely open. Naomi said, "I'm going to perform a little experiment on your body. Okay? I don't know if it'll work, but I know it's going to hurt. If it works, it's going to hurt like hell."

In a monotonous tone, Mario said, "I never 'experimented' on your husband. An eye for an eye... The law of retaliation... You're breaking all of the rules."

"I know, I know. I understand that, but I still have to punish you. Besides, sometimes it's not about an eye for an eye or a tooth for a tooth. Trades aren't always equal, so, this time, it's about a face for an arm."

Grimacing, Mario looked down at the coffee table and cried, "That's not fair..."

"Life isn't fair. I learned that a long time ago. You actually taught me that."

Naomi crouched beside his chair. She placed her left hand on his right deltoid muscle, her ring and middle fingers spread wide. Then, she placed the drill bit between her ring and middle fingers.

Mario took a deep breath through his nose and closed his eye. He was certain there was nothing he could do to stop her, so he gave up.

Naomi gritted her teeth, squeezed the trigger, and pressed the spinning drill *into* his deltoid muscle. The drill entered his arm, causing blood to spray every which way. The blood even splattered on Naomi's face and entered her mouth, but she didn't stop. She just spit the blood out, never taking her eyes off his mangled arm.

Mario didn't want to resist Naomi's torture. He just wanted to die and move on. He wasn't immune to pain, though. The drill twisted and tore through his muscle. Along with a plentiful amount of blood, strands of his fibrous muscle and veins—or what looked like veins—dangled out of his arm and reached down to his elbow. He looked up at the ceiling and screamed.

Naomi stopped drilling around two-and-a-half inches into his muscle. She narrowed her eyes and examined the hole on his arm. *Good enough,* she thought.

His head slumped down to his chest, Mario panted as he watched Naomi. His breaths were fast and hoarse, his eye was hollow and listless. He thought: *kill me, just kill me.*

Naomi walked back to her backpack. As she riffled through her supplies, she said, "I had a hard time getting my hands on that revolver. It's not as easy as it looks these days. You can't just buy a gun from a shady guy in a van in an alley, either. No, life isn't a movie. Life has rules and consequences. It was much easier getting the ammunition, though. I just had to walk into an 'authorized' seller, asks for the cartridges, show my ID, then pay. That's it. Simple, right?"

Naomi pulled a single 12-gauge shotgun shell out of the bag. She approached Mario while wagging the shell at him. Mario shuddered with fear as soon as he spotted the shell. He didn't see a shotgun in the room, so his imagination ran wild with the possibilities.

Before he could utter a word, Naomi shoved the shotgun shell into the wound on his arm. Mario hissed as she twisted her wrist and screwed the shell into the wound until only the brass head of the shell protruded from his arm.

Naomi said, "I've seen people do this on YouTube. Some kids clamp down an empty cartridge or a shell like this one, then they hit it and watch it explode. There's a big difference here, though—a *very big* difference. You see, this shell is *not* empty and it's *inside* of your arm. So, what do you think will happen when I hit the primer?"

It will explode in my arm—Mario knew the answer, but he couldn't utter those words. He didn't know why, he wasn't an overly superstitious person, but he feared it would come true if he responded. He sniffled and trembled, anxiously waiting for the experiment to fail or succeed. Either way, he knew pain was inevitable.

Naomi walked back to the sofa and reached into her backpack. She pulled a steel hammer and a steel chisel out of the bag.

She returned to Mario's side and said, "Here goes nothing..."

She held the chisel in her left hand and the hammer in the other. She held the tip of the blade over the shell's primer with a steady hand. Then, she leaned back and moved her head as far away from Mario as possible. If the shell actually exploded in his arm, she didn't want the pellets to strike her. *Here it goes,* she thought.

Mario kept his eye on his wife. He spotted Naomi's shadow on the floor. He saw her lifting the hammer over her shoulder. He closed his eye and thought: *just let me die already.*

Naomi screamed and swung the hammer down. She struck the butt of the chisel, which caused the blade to hit the primer. *Nothing.* The gunpowder didn't ignite, the shot didn't exit the cartridge.

Naomi nervously laughed and shook her head,

blatantly unnerved by the experience. She expected deadly projectiles to shoot out in every direction. Mario let out an exhale of relief and cried, causing gooey saliva to drip from his mouth. He knew it wasn't over, though. The tension was thick in the room, smothering both of them.

Naomi said, "Okay. Let's try this again."

Barely negligible, Mario muttered, "Do it. Do it already, damn it."

Once again, Naomi held the chisel over the primer and the hammer over her shoulder. She took a deep breath, then she swung the hammer down. The hammer hit the chisel and the chisel hit the primer with a *clink* sound. The cartridge ignited in his arm with a *banging* sound. The pellets shot out in every direction inside *and* outside of his arm.

Naomi fell back on the floor, shocked by the detonation. The hammer and chisel slipped out of her hands. A few pellets struck her arm and torso, penetrating her clothing and skin. Blood soaked through her layers of jackets. The wounds, however, were not fatal. Although the pellets broke her skin, her vital organs and arteries remained unharmed.

Mario's arm, on the other hand, was mangled by the detonation. The pellets tore through the rest of his muscle, driven deep into his flesh. He felt the pellets in his body, too. He couldn't ignore them. The center of his deltoid muscle was blown away. His exposed flesh resembled mushy ground meat. The tiny, three-quarter-inch hole on his arm became a bloody crater. It looked as if his arm were barely connected to the rest of his body by a tiny piece of flesh.

Mario slowly turned his head and glanced over at his mangled arm. He let out a broken, horrified breath. *She actually blew my arm off,* he thought, *how the hell did this happen?* He wheezed and groaned as he looked away. His head spun and his eyelids flickered. He went unconscious, he awoke, he went unconscious, and then he awoke again because of the shock and pain. It was a jarring experience.

As she struggled to her feet, one hand over the wounds on her stomach, Naomi said, "I can't believe that worked. I started planning this weeks ago and... and I can't believe it worked."

She chuckled and rubbed Mario's bald head. Somehow, a droplet of blood managed to land on the very top of his head. Mario couldn't muster the energy to respond. He was rapidly losing blood, so he was barely staying conscious. Along with plenty of his own blood, a cold sweat drenched his body, so he felt hot and cold at the same time.

Naomi sat down on the armrest of the sofa. She said, "That was... intense. We've reached the end of the line, though. The sun will rise in less than an hour. So, there's only one thing left to do. You know what I'm talking about, don't you?" Mario didn't respond. Naomi said, "It's only right that this night ends in a fashion that resembles the 'event' that started it all."

Again, Mario did not respond. He thought about his life and his family as his head swayed left and right. Life and all of its cruel tricks amazed him. Yesterday, he ate breakfast with his family, he kissed them, he went to work, and he spent time with his employees. Through the night and early morning, on the other hand, he was tortured and his family was slaughtered. *Life isn't fair,* he thought, *I always knew that, so how did I forget it?*

Naomi asked, "Are you ready for this? Are you ready to–"

Tap, tap, tap—knocking echoed through the home. Only the sound of dripping blood followed.

Naomi glared at the front door and said, "Now who the hell is that?"

Chapter Seventeen

Out of Time

Before he could utter more than a groan, Naomi lunged forward and covered Mario's mouth with the strip of tape. She held her index finger over her lips —*shh.* She grabbed the revolver, then she flicked a switch on the wall and turned off the living room lights. Her victims were swallowed by the darkness.

She thought: *three bullets, I have to make them count.* She crept up to the front door, stepping as quietly as possible.

Tap, tap, tap—the knocking came from the front door again, faster and louder. Her uninvited guest was clearly eager to get inside.

From the porch, a man said, "Redwood Police Department, open up."

Naomi whispered, "Shit."

She stood on her tiptoes and peeked through the peephole. She bit her bottom lip and shook her head, disappointed. A blonde-haired, blue-eyed police officer stood on the porch, one hand hovering over his holstered handgun. He was a young guy, but he could easily overpower her if she unlocked the door. She couldn't take that risk.

With a pinch of uncertainty in her voice, Naomi asked, "Who is it?"

The officer shouted, "My name is Dennis Cooper! I'm with the Redwood Police Department. Open up, ma'am."

"I'm sorry, um... We didn't call the police, sir."

"I didn't say you called the police. We've received multiple noise and smell complaints."

"Oh, well, we've been having a wild night. We had a... a barbecue. There were a few drinks, some furniture was broken, but everything's fine. You can go."

The officer scratched his brow and said, "Ma'am, you have to open the door. This is being treated as a domestic disturbance and the state treats these calls very seriously. It doesn't matter who called, I have to check up on everyone and everything. So, open the door."

Naomi weaved and bobbed her head as she peeked through the peephole, checking every angle. *Only one cop,* she thought, *I can handle him.* She lifted the revolver and tried to aim at him through the door.

She said, "I'm sorry, sir. My hands are tied at the moment."

She watched as the officer took three steps back. He spoke into the radio on his shoulder and updated the dispatcher while his other hand touched his holster. He took cover around the corner.

Dennis shouted, "Open the door, ma'am!"

Naomi yelled, "Fine! I'm opening the door!"

Still looking through the peephole, Naomi loudly turned the locks, ensuring the officer heard her. The cop moved away from his cover and approached the door again, believing he defused the situation. Naomi took three steps back, then she squeezed the trigger. She fired all three rounds through the door.

One bullet struck the officer's lower abdomen,

another struck his chest at the collarbone, and the other *whooshed* past him. He wasn't wearing a vest, so the bullets easily penetrated his torso. He collapsed on the porch, blood spouting from his wounds.

Naomi rushed forward and quickly opened the door. She was out of ammunition, but she still aimed the revolver at the cop.

Naomi kicked his arm before he could reach his handgun. She said, "Don't reach for it, don't fight me. I *will* blow your brains out." She pulled the handgun out of his holster, then she shoved it into the back of her waistband. She said, "Don't do anything stupid, Dennis. It's not worth it. Your family needs you to stay alive. Okay?"

Grunting and groaning between every other word, Dennis responded, "Don't... do it. Please, don't... don't kill me."

"I won't. I can't. God needs you to live, Dennis. You must survive in order to join us in the fight against the demons. He told me so. His word is true. It's so true."

Dennis' eyes welled with tears and veins protruded from his red face. He stared up at Naomi, baffled by her speech. He thought: *what is she talking about? What has she done?* Naomi walked past him. She grabbed the collar of his shirt, then she pulled him off the porch and dragged him across the walkway—all while aiming the empty revolver at his head.

She left him near the front gate and said, "Call for backup. Everyone has to see what I've done."

Naomi gazed into Dennis' eyes, as if she were

uncertain about something. She sighed, then she walked away from the cop. She returned to the house, closing and locking the door behind her.

As she removed the tape from Mario's mouth, she said, "Show's over. This place will be swarming with cops in a few minutes. You know how it is when a cop is shot, don't you? Depending on how trigger happy they are, it could end badly for me. I'm crossing my fingers and hoping for the best, though."

Mario remained quiet. He breathed throatily, but he didn't say a word. He was dazed and devastated by his loss of blood and the loss of life. He didn't have anything else to say to Naomi anyway. He simply waited for his inevitable death.

Naomi said, "I don't believe you were ever sick. I don't think you were truly mentally ill. Like I've been saying all night, I think you were just a psycho who wanted to kill. But, I tortured you and I killed your family so we're even now. You are forgiven."

Mario didn't respond, but he heard Naomi's words. *Forgiveness,* he thought, *what good is forgiveness if it comes after vengeance?*

Naomi continued, "I learned a lot during this process. I learned about myself, about people, about love. Vicky and Layla, they were good people. They really loved you, even after knowing about your nasty crime. It's amazing what love does to the mind, isn't it? I guess that's why some people never leave their abusers... They're sick with love, huh? Anyway, I'm sorry about killing them, but I had to do it. There was something inside of me that just... that made me do it, you know? I guess you can say a voice in my head told me to do it."

Mario looked up at her. He was insulted by the implication. *She's going to try to pretend to be sick,* he thought, *that evil bitch.* He imagined Naomi at her future court cases, fooling everyone thanks to her tragic past. He thought about exacting his revenge against her and creating a never-ending cycle of vengeance. He knew it was impossible, though. He thought: *if she gets away with it, no one will be around to punish her.* He lowered his head and cried, tears plopping on his mutilated thighs.

Naomi pulled a boning knife out of the bag. The knife had a dull, rusty blade and it wasn't serrated. It worked, though.

Teary-eyed, she approached Mario and said, "Let's see if I can finish what you tried to do to Trevor." She pushed his head back, put the blade to his neck, and sternly asked, "Are you ready, you sick son of a bitch?"

Mario clenched his jaw and nodded—*do it.* While holding the top of his head with her left hand, Naomi gritted her teeth and sawed into his neck with the knife. A tearing sound—like thin fabric being torn—dominated the room as she moved the blade back-and-forth across his thick neck. She severed his jugular, which caused blood to squirt onto her face.

One inch, two inches, *three inches*—she created a gash that was three inches deep on his neck with the blade. Blood gushed out from the gash, soaking his tank top and drenching his shoulder.

As she sawed into him, images of Trevor flashed in Naomi's mind. She saw him at the Peacock's Beer & Lounge. She saw him at the hospital on the day of Riley's birth. Then, although she never actually saw him at the scene of the crime, she saw him sitting at the back of the blood-soaked bus— dead and horribly disfigured. The images of Trevor gave her the strength to continue.

Five inches—the blade was driven five inches into his neck, passing the center of his throat at an angle.

Mario clenched his jaw, shook on the chair, and gritted his teeth until they cracked. He couldn't stop himself from trembling. The tape around his body couldn't stop him, either. *Gurgling* and *popping* sounds escaped from his mouth along with his panicked breaths. He struggled to breathe through his ruptured airway. He closed his one good eye, grimacing in pain. His hands shook, waving left and right. He tried to clench his fists, but he could only move a few of his fingers.

As the rusty blade cut through his neck, Mario thought about his life and his family. He spent the night thinking about the past—*repenting* for his past sins. He knew it was wrong to kill Trevor and he knew, in some twisted way, Naomi's vengeance was justified. He destroyed her family, so she destroyed his. Yet, he also *stopped* regretting his actions. If he didn't kill Trevor, he wouldn't have formed such a lovely family with Vicky. He was grateful for the time he spent with his family.

Mario's chair fell over as the sound of wailing sirens surrounded the home. The attempted decapitation didn't end, though. Naomi mounted him and continued sawing into his neck, cutting through the muscles, tendons, and blood vessels. A geyser of dark blood shot up from his neck like water from a fountain. The knife came to a sudden stop, causing Naomi to lose her grip on the handle. The blade was jammed in his thick flesh.

Naomi staggered to her feet. She breathed heavily, struggling to catch her breath. She watched as Mario twitched and groaned. She examined the wound on his neck. A *hissing* sound emerged from the gash, as if he were leaking some sort of gas through his throat. She saw every tint of red and pink in the cut, and even some white. *Bones?*–she thought. She was curious, but it didn't bother her very much. She was ready to move forward with the decapitation.

She lifted her right knee to her stomach, then she stomped on the knife's handle. One stomp wasn't enough—it was *never* enough. She stomped the handle five times. With each stomp, the blade sank deeper into his neck and even broke through his vertebrae.

Mario passed away with the first stomp, though. His last thought was simple but sincere: *I'm sorry.* Naomi just didn't notice his death. She kicked at his neck a few more times, then she stomped on his head—*thud, thud, thud.* Gashes formed on his temple, his forehead, his cheek, and his jaw. His skull was nearly caved in by her heavy boot.

After a minute, Naomi stopped stomping on him. She cried and mumbled indistinctly as she walked backwards. She bumped into the coffee table, then she fell onto the sofa.

Over the sound of the sirens outside, she shouted, "You bastard!"

Chapter Eighteen

The Voice of God

The sun rose beyond the horizon, painting the clear sky with tints of blue and yellow. Sirens blared through the area, announcing the arrival of the police. Some police cruisers cordoned off the street, blocking and redirecting traffic. A few officers evacuated the neighbors from their houses while others prepared themselves to raid the Flores home.

Mario remained on the floor, attached to his chair with a knife protruding from his neck. His disfigured face, drenched in blood, was unidentifiable. Her jaw dangling open, Vicky's body stayed on the other chair. Her skin was pale, her eyelids were dark, her body was stiff. Layla's burnt body still emitted a vile stench, staining every room in the house with the aroma of death.

Naomi sat on the sofa, holding one hand over her mouth. She sniffled and whimpered as she stared vacantly at Mario's dead body. She could hear the sirens outside. She even heard the police chatter on the street, shuffling as they moved into their positions. At heart, the uncertainty of the situation terrified her the most, though.

The possibilities were frightening. The police could gun her down in the house—*shoot first, ask questions later.* It seemed plausible, especially if Officer Dennis Cooper died on his way to the hospital. She could be arrested, which could lead to several different punishments. Freedom didn't seem like a likely outcome.

Naomi nervously laughed and wiped the tears from her cheeks. She took a deep breath, she held it in for a few seconds, then she slowly exhaled. She repeated the process five more times, acting as if she were preparing herself for a live performance. The calm, controlled breathing helped her control her anxiety.

She whispered, "It's time to put it to the test." She stood from her seat and glanced up at the ceiling. She said, "I love you, Trevor. I love you, Riley. Please watch over me."

Blood splattered on her face and clothes, Naomi shambled to the front door. She stood on her tiptoes and peeked through the peephole. The front lawn appeared to be empty. Police cruisers weren't parked in front of the house, either. She knew the cops were out there, though. She grabbed the door knob. She thought: *this is it.* She took one final deep breath, then she opened the door.

Naomi's eyes narrowed to a squint as a wave of sunshine poured into the house. To her utter surprise, the police didn't rush her. A hail of bullets didn't rain down on her, either. She walked onto the porch with her hands raised over her head. Her breathing intensified upon spotting the blood on the walkway. One question echoed through her mind: *are cops as vengeful as I am?*

As soon as she stepped onto the walkway, a male cop yelled, "Get down on the ground! Now!"

Wide-eyed, Naomi glanced over to her left. Police officers were lined up on the lawn of the neighboring house. A cop with a ballistic shield stood at the front of the line, selflessly defending his peers. They aimed their handguns at her, ready to shoot at a moment's notice.

"Get down!" another male officer barked. He shouted, "Get down on your knees! Don't make any sudden movements!"

Naomi looked over to her right, amazed. In a similar formation, another group of police officers stood on the front lawn of the other neighbor's house. One of the officer's even aimed a rifle at her. Since the space between the houses was wide, the officers were far away from the house. She clearly caught them off guard with her unexpected surrender.

Due to the possible crossfire, Naomi assumed they wouldn't shoot. She seized the opportunity and began the show.

Naomi looked up at the sky and shouted, "God! God, my lord, my savior, my master! I have done what you asked of me! I have slain the demon, I have slaughtered his kin! They will never hurt anyone again!"

"Get down on the fucking ground!" an officer yelled.

At the top of her lungs, Naomi shouted, "This city has been purged, lord! Take us to your kingdom! Begin the Rapture!" She cracked a smile and tears rolled down her cheeks. She whispered, "I just want to see my family again. Take me to them."

The cops shouted different variations of the same demands: *get down on the ground! Put your hands on your head! Don't reach for anything!*

Naomi ignored their demands. Their voices faded away, reduced to muffled whispers. With dozens of firearms aimed at her, she seriously thought about dying—suicide by cop. It wasn't part of the plan, but death actually seemed welcoming. *Just a few minutes of pain,* she thought, *then I can go away and join them.*

She sighed and shook her head. She murdered an entire family in order to make a point. From the beginning of the night, she had planned on faking her insanity in order to avoid a prison sentence. She believed Mario faked his mental illness, so she planned on doing the same. She couldn't allow Vicky and Layla to die in vain, either. She fell to her knees with her fingers interlocked behind her head.

As an officer pushed her to the ground, his knee on her back, Naomi shouted, "You're making a mistake! You're interfering with God's plan, you fool! His voice, the voice of the Almighty, told me to slay that demon! Don't you see? Can't you hear him calling us to his kingdom?"

She giggled maniacally as the police surrounded her. She continued to babble about the voices in her head as they pulled her arms back and handcuffed her. They dragged her away from the house and threw her in the back of a police cruiser.

"Get her to the station," an officer ordered.

From the backseat of the car, Naomi watched as a group of cops entered the Flores house. She could only imagine the shock and awe on their faces when they stumbled upon the massacre. A young, bald-headed cop climbed into the driver's seat of the car. He appeared to be flustered by the situation. He pulled out of the side of the road and headed to the station.

A sly smirk on her face, Naomi leaned closer to the cage partition and asked, "Have you heard the voice of God? Hmm? Are you ready for the Rapture?"

Join the mailing list!

Are you a fan of dark, disturbing, and provocative horror? Do you enjoy exploring taboo subjects? Would you like to read more books like *Sympathy for the Widow?* If you answered 'yes' to any of those questions, you should join my mailing list. I publish an extreme horror book nearly every month—sometimes I even publish two in a single month. By signing up for my mailing list, you'll receive an email whenever I release a new book and you'll also be the first to know about deep discounts. Best of all, the process requires very little effort and it's completely *free.*

By signing up, you'll only receive 1-2 emails per month. If I'm having a very big sale, you *might* receive three emails a month, but that's usually not necessary. You won't get any spam, either. Click here to sign-up: http://eepurl.com/bNI1CP

Dear Reader,

Hello! Thanks for reading *Sympathy for the Widow*. This was a *very* violent book, wasn't it? I'd say it's one of the most violent books I've ever written—and I've written more than a few violent novels. And, of course, when things are violent or taboo, some people will be outraged. There were **warnings** on the book—on the back of the paperback, in the front matter, and on the product page—but I'm sure someone, somewhere, was offended. If you were offended because you either stumbled upon this book by mistake or because you ignored the warnings, I apologize. Honestly, I don't write to offend or hurt people. I write to terrify and to evoke certain emotions.

This book was *partially* inspired by real crimes— the first chapter, at least. It was inspired by crimes committed by people with mental illness. The purpose wasn't to criticize, shun, or hurt them, though. I used these criminals and their crimes as a starting point because it fed into a theme I wanted to write about: *sympathy for killers.* Although the book is titled *Sympathy for the Widow,* I tried to make you sympathize, or at least empathize, with both of the main characters.

While I was conducting my research for this book, I thought: *what would I do if a loved one were killed and the killer were set free? What would I do if that killer were a person with a mental illness? Would I still feel the same? Would I want vengeance?*

Obviously, I've thought a lot about vengeance in my life—I've written a few books on the subject, in fact —so that immediately came to mind. I felt like this idea created an interesting and compelling concept.

More importantly, I wanted *you,* the reader, to ask yourself a few questions. Should a person with mental illness who commits a violent crime be punished or treated? How would you feel if you were placed in Naomi's situation? What if someone you loved were the victim of a similar crime? Do you believe in an 'eye for an eye?' Or could you let it all go and move on with life? In terms of this story, do you blame Naomi or Mario? Is anyone to blame? And, the big question is: after all was said and done, did you have sympathy for the widow? It's a very difficult situation, right? Well, that's what I hoped to create. I'm sure some readers will dismiss this as just another 'splatter novel,' and that's okay, but I really put a lot into it. I hope you can see that.

By the way, this book was also partially inspired by Park Chan-wook's *Lady Vengeance.* If you haven't watched it, check it out. It's a great movie.

Okay, now it's time to beg for reviews. If you enjoyed this book, *please* leave a review on Amazon.com. It may not seem like much, but it is *very* helpful. Your reviews help me improve on my writing, it helps me decide what to write next, and it helps other readers find this book. Good or bad, your reviews lead to more books—*better books.* They also help me live. If you need help, here are some questions you can answer to get you started. Did you enjoy the story? Did you connect to the characters? Did the story terrify you? Were you moved by the themes? Was this a provocative experience? Would you like to see more books like these in the future? Answering questions like this will help me understand you.

Want to show even more support? Post a link to this book on Facebook or Twitter, share the awesome book cover on Instagram or Snapchat, write a post about it on your blog, buy a paperback for yourself or a friend, or buy a Kindle copy for a distant friend/relative. By the way, if you buy a paperback of *any* of my books, you get a free Kindle version, too. Great deal, right? Sharing books is an excellent way to support independent authors. It's a great way to make new friends, too. People love good books—and I hope this one was good enough to share.

So, how am I doing these days? In regards to health, I think I'm fine. (*'Think'* is the keyword in that sentence.) Financially, I'm... okay. I'm not rolling in dough, my pockets aren't stuffed with cash and credit cards, but I'm doing okay. I'm fortunate enough to have shelter and I can afford to pay my bills. I hope I can go on a vacation/work-trip soon, especially with some of the upcoming novels I have planned. We'll see what happens. Your support has been very helpful, though. Thank you very much for everything you've done for me, even if this is the first book of mine that you've read.

Finally, if you're a horror fan, feel free to visit my Amazon's Author page. I've published nearly two dozen horror novels, a few sci-fi/fantasy books, and some anthologies. Want to read a shocking story of adolescence, friendship, envy, and horror? Check out *Our Dead Girlfriend.* Looking for another disturbing story of human horror? Check out next month's release, *At Grandfather's House.* If you're new to my work, please feel free to check out some of my older novels, too. Some of them are actually pretty good according to reviewers. If you've read them all already, you're an awesome person. You know this already, too: I release a new book every month, so another one will be out soon. Once again, thank you for reading. Your readership keeps me going through the darkest times!

Until our next venture into the dark and disturbing,
Jon Athan

P.S. If you have questions (or insults), you can contact me through my business email: *info@jon-athan.com.* I love hearing from readers, even if it's just a short comment. You can also contact me via Twitter @Jonny_Athan or my Facebook page. Thanks again!